I ESCAPED PIRATES IN THE CARIBBEAN

ELLIE CROWE

SCOTT PETERS

I Escaped Pirates In The Caribbean (I Escaped Book Seven)

Library of Congress Control Number:

ISBN: 978-1951019204 (Hardcover)

ISBN: 978-1951019198 (Paperback)

Book cover design by Susan Wyshynski

Best Day Books For Young Readers

Port Royal, Jamaica
The Year 1671

White sails billowed. Fifteen-year-old Jon stood on the deck of the pirate sloop, the *Fury*, and scanned the ocean. The green mountains of Jamaica rose on the horizon. This was his chance.

His fists clenched the ship's bulwark. He was going to escape, hide in the jungle until the pirates left, and beg his way onto a merchant ship. Escape, or die trying.

Blackheart Bill, seven-foot-tall and mean as a piranha, rattled the silver coins in his pockets. "Nearly there. I've got plenty to spend this time, too." He shot Jon a shark-like sneer. "And more coming."

Jon winced. He and his friend Fortune had almost perished getting those silver coins, and Blackheart Bill had pocketed them all.

"Revenge would be sweet," Fortune muttered.

"Freedom would be sweeter." Jon studied Port Royal's harbor. By himself, he could leap over the side and make it to shore.

But Fortune couldn't swim.

"As soon as we're ashore," he whispered, "get ready to run."

Captain Morgan shouted, "Drop anchor!"

Pirates jostled, all eager to get to shore. Nerves hopping, Jon lined up behind Fortune, keeping a watch for Blackheart Bill.

Without warning, steely fingers sank into his arm. The massive pirate was right behind him.

"You're coming to the ship's hold with me," Blackheart Bill said.

"We're not." Jon's heart raced wildly. "We're getting off in Port Royal."

"Oh no you're not, ye thumb-sucking pups," the pirate snarled. "You'll stay aboard until your parents pay me my ransom."

"That's not fair!" Fortune shouted.

Throwing back his head, Blackheart Bill laughed. "Pirates are never fair. Surely ye know that by now."

The Caribbean Sea
The Year 1670
Three Months Previously

Tall masts creaked. Ropes cracked like cannon fire. The proud English merchant ship dipped and surged through the stormy sea. The *Princess*—a two-mast vessel manned by trusty English sailors—was filled to bursting with trade goods bound for the Caribbean islands. Grain, beef, tobacco, textiles, and building supplies filled its hull.

Jon let out a mighty whoop. At last, he was on the high seas!

It was unbelievable.

Running away to become a merchant sailor was the best thing he'd ever done.

Up the ship went, lifted by another huge wave. Down it slid into a deep, watery valley, Jon's stomach dropping with it.

Holding the rail, he tented a hand across his brow and squinted up at the crow's nest. The small barrel, fastened tightly to the top of a mast, swayed dizzily with the rocking ship. And inside sat his friend, Fortune.

A skinny shrimp of thirteen, Fortune made a pretty good barrelman—he could climb up and down that mast like a monkey. He'd sit up there for hours, keeping an eye out for land, ships, and other dangers. There was only one problem—Fortune got seasick.

"See anything?" Jon called to his friend.

Fortune didn't reply. Instead, he kept the spyglass pressed to one eye, studying a point on the horizon.

"Hey, Fortune!" Jon shouted. "What's going on up there?"

"I'm going to puke," Fortune shouted. "The ship is swaying like a drunken sailor."

Jon grinned. "Don't puke on me!"

He couldn't work out why Fortune had become a seaman. Sure, being small made him the perfect size to fit in the crow's nest. And he was a good climber. But along with getting seasick, he hated getting wet.

Jagged lightning forked across the dark sky.

A moan came from the crow's nest.

"Don't spew on the poop deck," Jon shouted. "I mean it, I don't want to clean that up."

"Don't worry, you won't have to. Here comes the rain. A huge storm's rolling in," Fortune yelled. "And I mean huge!"

The sky grew dim, the clouds blotting out the sun. A wave rose up. Like black glass, it crashed over the bow.

Water surged around Jon's feet, trying to knock him off balance. He tightened the safety rope holding him to the rail and braced his feet against the slanting deck. Sailing sure was exciting.

"Disable the masts. Haul in the shrouds," the captain shouted. "Batten the hatches."

"Aye aye, sir." Jon joined the other seamen as they leaped into action.

He wished his pa could see him. Pa was a whaler. He'd promised to take Jon to sea when Jon turned fifteen. But then Ma said whaling was too dangerous. Pa had sailed away, leaving Jon at home still dreaming of the ocean.

But Jon hadn't stayed home for long.

Three nights after Pa left, Jon kissed Ma goodnight, patted Tucker, the family dog, climbed out his bedroom window, and headed to Charles Town, a bustling new colony settlement. At the wharf, he'd joined the crew of the merchant sailing ship, the *Princess*.

This was the life he wanted. Sure, he was just a ship's boy now, but he was learning fast. When they reached Jamaica, maybe he'd join the Royal Navy as a midshipman. Or a gunner. The gunners protected England's Caribbean islands from Spanish attacks—that would be really exciting.

Now, a sudden burst of rain poured down Jon's neck. Fog blanketed the ocean, making it hard to see. The crew worked to keep the ship steady in the pounding storm.

Up in the crow's nest, Fortune shouted, "Ship ho! Starboard!"

Ship ho? Was a boat coming? In this mess?

Brown hair whipping his face, Jon squinted toward the starboard side. Like a phantom, a dark vessel emerged from the fog.

"What flag's she under?" the captain shouted up to him.

"I can't see."

"Well, what can you see, barrelman?"

"Cannons!" Fortune cried. "They're aiming cannons at us! They're loading fire!"

The captain began yelling orders.

Fortune slid down the ratlines and grabbed Jon's arm. "We're done for!"

Zounds! Fortune was right. The enemy ship was close enough to see her open gun-ports.

"Barrelman!" the quartermaster roared as men armed themselves. "Were you asleep up there?"

"It snuck up, sir," Fortune babbled. "Like a shark in the night."

"And you saw no flag? What is she?" the quartermaster demanded. "Spanish?"

Jon peered into the fog. If it was Spanish, they were done for. A cargo-laden vessel like the *Princess* was a juicy prize.

Spain would fight like the devil to get her hands on it. The *Princess* stood no chance of victory against a well-armed naval ship.

"Gunners! To your stations!" the captain shouted.

"Look!" Fortune screamed, his panicked voice rising above the sea's angry roar.

"What is it?" Jon yelled.

"The flag. They're raising their flag!"

Then Jon saw it, and it didn't belong to Spain. The flying standard was black, marked in its center with a menacing white skull and crossbones.

A Jolly Roger.

"Pirates!" Fortune screamed. "They're pirates!"

"All hands on deck!" the captain cried. "Gunners, load the cannons! Save our souls. It's the pirate ship *Satisfaction*. She's manned by the blood-thirstiest pirate in the Caribbean—Captain Morgan! To your stations!"

The menacing ship surged toward them, closing the distance, bearing down on the scrambling *Princess* crew.

But everything seemed to be happening in slow motion. Why weren't Jon's crewmates loading the cannons? Why was it taking so long? Jon had no clue what to do. They hadn't practiced an emergency drill. He'd only been on a ship for a few days, and already they were under attack.

The pirate ship was a mere two hundred feet away and closing fast. Jon gulped as a massive, black-bearded pirate grinned at him and let out a deep belly laugh. *Captain Morgan!*

A second pirate, his arm rippling with a snake tattoo, tossed a grappling hook attached to a thick rope across the water. The rope whizzed, and the hook latched onto the *Princess* with an awful *THUNK.*

It startled Jon into action. "They're boarding!"

"A musket, boy, take it!" a sailor growled, shoving the weapon into Jon's hands.

Jon had never fired a musket. If only he had Pa's hunting rifle!

More grappling hooks latched onto their ship. Pirates whooped and began swinging across.

Jon steadied his aim and fired. The shot went wide.

Swords in hand, cutlasses between their teeth, the pirates landed on deck and began lunging and thrusting at the poor crewmen. It was clear few of the Princess's crew knew how to fight.

"Surrender, ye scurvy dogs, or we'll sink ye!" Captain Morgan yelled.

"We're not surrendering," shouted Jon's captain, his voice gruff with desperation. "Seamen! Prepare to fight."

The *Princess'* seamen rallied. Gunners loaded grapeshot. Muskets fired. Red-hot, glowing fireballs flew overhead. Swords clashed.

"Where's the powder monkey?" yelled the quartermaster. "We need more gunpowder for the guns!"

Fortune appeared at Jon's side. "They're slaughtering

us," he babbled. "We're fish food! Jon! We've gotta get out of here!"

"And go where?"

Fortune didn't answer. Instead, the skinny shrimp bolted. Fast as a rat fleeing a sinking ship, he threw himself overboard. Through the air he dove, straight into the thundering sea.

"Fortune!" Jon shouted. "You can't swim, you nincompoop!"

A pirate lunged. With no time for a better plan, Jon slid across the wet deck, scrambled over the bulwark, and plunged into the ocean to join his friend.

D own Jon went. Deep into the black ocean.
Luckily, he'd learned to swim off Charles Town
beach. Kicking furiously, he popped to the surface.

"Help!" Fortune floundered in the churning waves.
"Help!"

Jon kicked his way to him.

Fortune's arms locked around Jon's neck, hanging on
like a madman. The skinny, little lad was stronger than he
looked.

"You'll drown us both! Let go!" Jon ripped his friend's
hands apart.

"Save me!" Fortune jabbered, gulping water.

A wave smacked them. Jon grabbed him by the shirt
and held on. They were tossed, tumbling around and
around until they slammed up against the pirate ship's
hull.

Jon gulped. Talk about the last place he wanted to go.

He pushed off as a large triangular shape sliced
through the ocean less than twenty yards away.

"Shark!" Fortune screamed. "Shark!"

They had to get out of the water.

A rope dangled from the pirate ship. He shoved the end at Fortune.

"Grab on," he said. "Quick! Climb up."

"No way," Fortune spluttered, eyeing the shark as it drew nearer.

"Fortune, hurry up! You climb ropes all the time."

"Onto the pirate ship? Are you crazy?"

Something bumped Jon's leg. Something big. "Sharks!" he yelled. "Look! More sharks! They're everywhere. Climb, you stupid nit!"

Fortune shimmied hand-over-hand up the rope.

Jon followed.

Gasping for breath, they flopped over the rail and scanned the pirate ship. Not a soul in sight. All the action was happening on the *Princess*, where gunfire boomed and swords clashed.

"We're goners," Fortune moaned.

"Just pray our captain wins the battle," Jon said. "We're sitting ducks here. We've got to hide."

Fortune covered his face and said, "It's worse for me. If they catch me, they'll string me up."

"You, why?" Jon said.

"Because I'm bad luck. That's what every seaman would say, pirate or not, if they knew the truth."

"What truth?"

"Jon, I've got a confession to make."

"Well, hurry up," Jon said, looking around wildly for a place to hide. Who cared about some stupid confession? "We're on a pirate ship. What could be worse than that?"

"I'm a girl."

Jon stared in shock. "You're a girl?"

"Yes. I am."

Fortune was a girl? He gulped. He'd brought a girl onto a pirate ship? Well, of course she was bad luck! Everyone knew having a woman aboard a ship brought bad luck. And pirates were the most superstitious of them all. If they found out, they'd toss her to the sharks before you could say walk the plank!

They'd probably do the same to Jon, just for being with her.

But Fortune was a friend. Jon wasn't about to leave him—er . . . *her*—in the lurch. Even if Fortune had been lying all this time.

"We can't get caught," Jon said.

"They're coming! Run. Behind those crates," she said.

"We'll be trapped aboard," Jon said. "We have to get back to the *Princess*!"

Still, they ran for cover as cheering pirates swung across the ropes, returning to the *Satisfaction*.

Peeking out between two large barrels, it was clear the pirates had won.

What had happened to the *Princess* crew? To the captain, quartermaster, and sailors? Had they perished in the fight?

Were Jon and Fortune alone?

Were they the only survivors?

The mystery of Jon and Fortune's crewmates was quickly solved. From behind their barrels, they watched as their shipmates were forced aboard the pirate ship.

Jon couldn't hear much, but it sounded like some kind of makeshift tribunal was underway. Captain Morgan was deciding who would be thrown in chains and kept for ransom and who would be forced into the pirate's service.

When that was done, Captain Morgan sent a small crew to man the *Princess* and sail it alongside the *Satisfaction*.

There was no escape now. Their whole ship had been captured. What would Captain Morgan do when he discovered two stowaways?

If only land was near. Jon could swim for it. But what of Fortune? He couldn't leave her behind. Anyway, they were in the middle of a wild and stormy sea, far from safe harbor.

As darkness fell, Jon and Fortune shivered from fear and cold.

"We've got to find a better hiding spot," Jon whispered. "Before it gets light."

"I know," Fortune whispered back.

Across the deck, pirates laughed, clinking jars of rum and singing pirate songs.

A gruff voice said, "We lost a good gunner, and Lazy-Eye Louie lost an ear. But we gained a fine ship."

"I'll drink to that, me mates," someone shouted. "And she's filled with rum, beer, grain, salt-fish, and tobacco. Gunpowder too. A good day's work!"

"She'll be part of our fleet," the gruff voice said. "Five fair ships we'll have now. It was a lucky storm that blew her our way."

"Lucky for us!" Someone gave a rumbling laugh. "And lucky the storm's gone. We've prisoners to ransom, too."

"Aye, mate, and Captain Morgan's gained us some strong men, besides. We'll make brothers of a couple of 'em yet. We have the luck of the devil himself!"

"I'll raise me jar of rum to that!"

More loud cheers rang out. "Here comes the captain!"

Unable to resist, Jon peeked around the barrel.

There he was, the bronze-skinned pirate Jon had seen before the attack. Tall, with long dark curls and a wicked grin, Captain Morgan strode along. Moonlight glinted on his gold earrings and the gilt-braid trimmings of his red coat. Pistols jutted from the pockets of his breeches and his cutlass sword shone at his waist.

Fortune whispered, "What's happening out there?"

"The pirate captain just showed up, and he's armed to the teeth."

Fortune nudged him sideways. "Let me see!"

"Shh!" Jon muttered, tense all the way to the roots of his hair. "You want to get caught?" Still, he moved so they both could see.

As the cheering stopped, Captain Morgan's deep voice rang out. "A fine night's work, me hearties! Are ye hungry, men?"

Something smelled good. Jon's stomach growled as a round-faced, curly-haired pirate in a dirty apron appeared. He plunked a steaming pot on a wooden table.

The cook gave a toothless grin. "Come and get it, m' lads!"

"Cook made turtle stew," shouted a red-bearded pirate.

The men dug in.

17

Jon's mouth watered.

"I'm starving," Fortune hissed. "We need to sneak food."

"No. We need to think of how to escape. We've got a lot of problems—like the fact that you're a girl! What were you doing on the *Princess*? Why did you even become a barrelman?"

Fortune scowled. "Mind your own business."

J on watched the men rubbing their full bellies and
wished his were full, too.

Suddenly, Cook shouted in alarm. "Look! On
that rock, me hearties. Do you see them? Mermaids!"

"Mermaids?" a pirate cried. "Where? Let me see!"

Bare feet and jackboots thudded across the deck.

Jon and Fortune scurried to the opposite side of the
barrel, keeping out of sight.

"Oh aye, Cook, I see them," a pirate gasped. "Their
green hair gleams in the moonlight. Like seaweed, it is."

"Bad luck, seeing them," Cook moaned. "They'll have
cursed us with trouble now, mark my words."

Jon nudged Fortune. "I told you they're superstitious."

Fortune put a finger to her lips.

"So beautiful." Cook's voice was full of longing. "But
vicious sea-devils. I saw mermaids once before. On a
whaling ship, it was."

"Did they lure men to their doom?" a pirate asked, his
voice hushed and shaky.

"Aye, Rusty Pete, that they did," Cook said. "They

were sitting pretty on a rock, singing: *Be with me, be with me.* And they reached out their arms to us, they did."

"What happened?" Rusty Pete asked.

"The sailors dove overboard and swam out to the she-devils. I was just a lad, but my pa had warned me well, so I lay down on the deck and clapped my hands over my ears. I couldn't shake the sound out of me head, though. Then I heard the sailors screaming."

"What? What happened to them?"

"I don't know," Cook said. "A wave took the ship and smashed it aground on that cursed rock. Down it went. I was the only survivor."

There was a moment of silence.

Jon and Fortune eyed one another. Was it true?

A new voice roared, "You're all a lot of scurvy idiots. Ye didn't see mermaids, Cook. What ye saw was seals."

Jon peeked out to see a hulking, black-bearded pirate with a patch over one eye and a mean-looking sneer.

"You calling me a liar?" Cook roared. "Ye scurvy, streak o' pee!" He dove across the deck. "Ye dirty, bilge-drinking rat! I'll kill you, Blackheart Bill!"

The two rolled around, raining blows on each other.

Blackheart Bill grabbed hold of Cook's head and dragged him to the bulwark. "Ye like them mermaids so much, ye can join them, ye jelly-belly whale!"

Cook let out a terrified scream.

Rusty Pete grabbed hold of Blackheart Bill's leg. "Pirate's Code," he shouted. "No brawling onboard."

The pirates pulled Cook and Blackheart Bill apart.

"That's more like it." A grinning pirate waved his hook. "Now bring on the rum, ye lily-livered dogs. We'll drink to a short life and a merry one."

Fortune snorted quietly in the dark. "Just be glad I'm a girl instead of a mermaid."

"A mermaid would be a lot more useful," Jon hissed back. "Then you could lure the pirates to their doom."

They sat in stony silence.

Jars clinked. Men roared with laughter. And Jon's stomach growled with hunger.

From the deck, a musician played accordion, and the pirates sang a sea shanty:

> *Fifteen men on a dead man's chest*
> *Yo ho ho and a bottle of rum*
> *Drink and the devil had done*
> *For the rest*
> *Yo ho ho and a bottle of rum.*

"How come you're dressed like a boy?" Jon whispered. "And how come you want to be a sailor when you hate sailing?"

Fortune winced. "I don't want to be a sailor, you nincompoop," she muttered. "I ran away from home. I was dressed like a boy because it was the only way I could get a job."

"On a boat?"

"No! I was a messenger boy, and I was doing all right, too. Until I got knocked on the head at the wharf. When I came to, I was aboard the *Princess* in the middle of the ocean. Can you believe it? They'd pressed me into service as the crew's barrelman. Talk about bad luck it was."

"Oh." Jon digested this strange story.

"Yes, my thoughts exactly," Fortune said.

"Why did you run away from home?"

Fortune sighed. "My papa died. And my mother married the meanest man in the whole world. He's a colonel and a bully. He's horrible to me, and he beats the slaves."

"That's awful." Jon thought of his parents. Even though Pa didn't take him on the whaling ship, Pa loved him, and Ma loved him, too. He felt terrible about leaving without saying goodbye. He decided to write his mother as soon as he reached Jamaica.

"We need a better hiding place," Fortune said.

"Yes, as soon as the pirates are asleep." Jon closed his eyes and tried to think up an escape plan.

He woke with a start.

Zookers! He'd fallen asleep, and dawn's light was creeping along the watery horizon. Were the pirates awake?

Overhead, the sails flapped in the breeze. Loud snores

filled the salty air. Jon peeked around the barrels. Hairy men lay sprawled across the deck, some in blankets, others in swaying hammocks.

He shook Fortune awake. "I'm going to scout for a better hiding place. Wait here. No need for us both to go creeping around."

She rubbed her eyes. "Fine."

He tiptoed to the ladder leading to the poop deck. An awful squeal made him spin around.

Fortune stood over the turtle stew pot, the ladle in her hand.

And the mean-looking pirate, Blackheart Bill, had her firmly by one arm.

Jon couldn't believe it. Talk about stupid! Trying to sneak turtle stew? And now they'd been caught by the nastiest, hugest pirate of them all.

Fortune plunged the ladle into the pot and sent goopy

liquid flying into Blackheart Bill's face. Startled, he lost hold of her arm. She raced down the galley way.

The massive pirate lunged after her.

Jon caught up as Blackheart Bill brought Fortune down in a tackle. They hit the deck, and Fortune's cap flew from her head. Her long hair fell into her eyes, but she kept fighting.

She yanked Blackheart Bill's beard, and he roared in agony. She sprang to her feet and delivered another well-aimed kick.

Wow! Girl or not, Fortune could really fight.

However, Blackheart Bill was bigger and stronger and grabbed her in a chokehold. Spinning her around, he stared into her face.

His eyes widened.

With her hair loose and tumbling down her back, Fortune looked precisely like what she was.

"Well, well. What do we have here?" Blackheart Bill snarled. "You're no boy! You're a perishing girl!"

J on rushed forward. "Let go of him!"

"*Him?* This is a *her*," Blackheart Bill said. "I knows me a girl when I see one."

Fortune scowled.

"I'm the quartermaster of this ship, and it's mighty sorry she'll be to have snuck aboard. Women are not allowed. Never."

Fortune straightened to her full height, which lay somewhere below Blackheart's armpit. "I didn't sneak onto your ship. You attacked the ship I was on."

Blackheart Bill snorted. "You're digging ye grave with ye tongue, ye nose-picking shrimp."

Maybe they should make another leap overboard, Jon thought.

Fortune spoke again. This time her voice was sweeter. Much sweeter. "You should know, good sir, that I am Lady Florabelle Rosewood of Rosewood Hall, Port Royal, Jamaica. My parents have oodles of money."

"Money, you say?"

"Loads of it. If you play your cards right, you could get yourself a nice reward. So take your dirty hands off me."

Jon blinked hard. What was Fortune up to? Surely Blackheart Bill would never fall for such nonsense.

But Blackheart Bill only scratched his armpit. "And what cards would those be? Speak fast, ye whining puppy, or I'll have you and yer friend here walking the plank." His muscles bulged, and his serpent tattoos writhed.

Fortune said, "If you keep it secret about me being a girl, I'll tell my parents you saved me. When we get to Port Royal, they'll pay you a big reward. You see, I was kidnapped and forced to wear boy's clothing for these long months. They will be terribly worried."

"Kidnapped, hey?" Blackheart Bill said.

"Yes. Now you'd like that big reward, wouldn't you?"

"Why should I believe you?" Blackheart Bill said, although his eyes shone with the promise of gold.

Jon spoke up. "Lady Florabelle's parents will be very grateful. She's their only child, and they love her dearly. They're one of Jamaica's richest families. Surely you've heard of them?"

Blackheart Bill rubbed his chin. "Hmm. We're not going

to Port Royal for a long time. Still ... we can cut a nice bargain, my moppets. On the next raid, I'll put you to work. You'll give me your cut of the booty. That's to pay me for my silence."

"Deal," Fortune said.

"And at Port Royal, I'll get my ransom—or I'll drown you like a pair of bilge-rats. One hundred pieces of silver. For each of you."

Jon sucked in his breath. That was an enormous sum. Could her parents afford it? Would they even pay it after she'd run away?

"Fine," Fortune said.

Jon had a bad feeling about this. But at least they'd bought themselves time.

Fortune tied her hair into a plait and hid it under her hat. "Now that's decided, I'd like some turtle stew."

Blackheart Bill snorted. "No." One hand on his cutlass, he marched Jon and Fortune up the ladder to the poop deck.

Ten familiar sailors from the *Princess* sat roped together in a corner. A burly pirate stood guard.

"Two more here, eager to learn the drill," Blackheart Bill said. "Add 'em to the holding pen."

"Aye, aye." The guard ordered Jon and Fortune to sit. He tied their ankles to the other prisoners.

Jon turned his back on her. Why did she have to go and get caught? All his life, he'd dreamed of whaling with his father or even of joining England's Royal Navy. Instead, he'd ended up a pirate's slave.

"Hello, my boy," said the grizzled navigator of the *Princess,* a man named Thomas. "Glad to see you're still alive."

"You, too, sir," Jon said. "But where are the rest of the *Princess'* crew?"

"In the hold."

"Why are you lot out here on the deck?" Jon asked.

The navigator gave a grim headshake. "I hear the pirates need more crew."

Blackheart Bill's voice rang out. "None of that talking or plotting ye sorry snot-rags."

At midday, Captain Morgan appeared. The famed pirate wore a feathered hat, a red embroidered waistcoat, canvas breeches, and mildewed knee-high jackboots. He studied the prisoners with calculating eyes.

"Greetings. I'm Captain Henry Morgan of the good ship *Satisfaction*," he said. "We Brethren of the Coast are on a mission, and there'll be gold and silver for the taking. All who wish to join us may do so."

Silence.

Captain Morgan donned a crooked smile. "I'll give you a choice: join me or be marooned on a sandbar. You'll not be forced."

One-by-one, the prisoners nodded in agreement. When Blackheart Bill glared at Jon and Fortune, they nodded, too.

"Excellent! Then welcome, men." Captain Morgan motioned at the guard. "Rusty Pete, untie our new brethren and explain the Pirate Code."

"Aye aye, Captain," Rusty Pete said, stroking his red beard.

Jon watched Captain Morgan march away.

He wondered if he'd ever make it back home to Ma and Pa.

"All right, gentlemen, I'm Rusty Pete," the pirate said. "Second Mate of the *Satisfaction*. It's a fine opportunity you're being given here. So, listen well. Once you sign the Pirate Code, you're sworn members of our band of brethren, and there's no turning back."

He waited for silence and continued. "We Brethren of the Coast fight together to the last drop of blood. We share the loot according to the Blades of Fortune. And we swear to never hide plunder from one another, not even one peso. Death to those who break our code."

To Jon's horror, he heard Fortune's voice.

"Sir, could you explain how the plunder is shared?"

Rusty Pete fingered his cutlass, then laughed. "Fair question m'lad. The captain gets the biggest share, five portions to what an ordinary seaman gets. Then the quartermaster takes his cut."

Blackheart Bill, who stood nearby, sneered at Jon.

"The rest is divided evenly between the crew," Rusty Pete continued. "But remember, no prey, no pay."

Jon and Fortune exchanged a glance. *No prey, no pay* .

. . Jon didn't like the sound of that, and apparently, Fortune didn't either.

"Now, here's the rules." Rusty Pete raised his fingers to count them out. "One, each man gets a vote on important matters. Two, no cowardice and no desertion. Three, no gambling aboard. Four, no shooting your brothers on deck, quarrels to be ended on shore, the victor be he who draws first blood. And five—" Rusty Pete's pinkie finger was missing, but he counted it anyway. "Most importantly, no women to be brought aboard."

At this, Blackheart Bill chuckled.

"What's the punishment for breaking the rules?" Jon asked.

"Depends. For shooting your brothers, we string ye up from the yardarm or give you forty stripes. Or maroon you on a sandbar with nothing but a jar of water and a pistol."

"What's the punishment for bringing a woman aboard?" Jon said.

"Shh!" Fortune hissed in his ear.

Rusty Pete eyed him carefully. "The penalty be to walk the plank."

Jon felt icy cold.

Cook had appeared. Now he piped up. "A woman angers the ocean, she does. There be terrible tales about unlucky ships that took a woman aboard. Like the mermaids, women be trouble."

Jon was glad when a fellow prisoner changed the subject.

"What if we're injured in battle?" the merchant sailor said.

Rusty Pete's face wrinkled in concentration. "For the loss of a right arm, ye get 600 pieces-of-eight or six slaves. For the loss of a left arm, ye get 500 pieces-of-eight or five slaves. For a right leg, ye get 500 pieces-of-eight or five slaves. For a left leg, 400 pieces-of-eight or four slaves. For an eye, 100 pieces-of-eight or one slave, and for a finger of the hand, the same as for the eye."

Wow, Jon thought, they really had that all worked out.

"Aye, our lives are rough," Rusty Pete said, rubbing the jagged scar on his forehead. "We risk swinging by the neck. But, me hearties, we drink like fighting cocks and we eat like pigs. And when a cruise is over, why it's pockets overflowing with Spanish silver. It's *Kill Devil Rum* by the flagon. It's a good fling with a pretty lass on each arm in Port Royal, the wickedest city in the world."

Cook grinned.

Rusty Pete produced a grubby parchment scroll. "Ye'll make your mark here, each one of you."

Several prisoners began to protest.

"Listen here, you scurvy dogs," Blackheart Bill snarled. "Spanish galleons are all around us, loaded with gold and silver, ripe for the plucking. They're enemies of the English Crown—remember that. We're doing the King's bidding."

Jon wasn't sure the King would see it that way.

Rusty Pete nodded. "You'll make more as a pirate, me hearties, than slaving for that stingy trader."

"I'll sign," called out the powder-monkey from the *Princess*, a freckle-faced boy. "I bet you need a good powder-monkey. Who else is going to dash around with the gunpowder?"

"Good lad," Blackheart Bill said.

"We have to sign," Fortune whispered, the wind tugging at her hat.

Jon nodded. "I know. Will your parents pay my ransom?"

"I doubt it. They may not even pay mine."

"Well, we won't hang around to find out. As soon as we get to Port Royal, we'll escape," Jon whispered.

"Agreed."

One by one, the prisoners nicked their left thumbs and pressed their mark in blood to the grubby parchment sheet.

"Welcome, gentlemen!" Rusty Pete handed each new pirate a jar of rum. "We're off to adventure and parts unknown. Down the hatch, and then it's off with you to scrub the battle scars from our new ship."

The prisoners-turned-pirates were ferried under guard back to the *Princess*, where they were handed buckets and brushes and ordered to swab the deck.

Thomas, the navigator, scrubbed alongside Jon.

"So," Thomas said with a sigh. "Looks like we're un-lucky brothers-in-arms."

"Sadly, it's even worse for Fortune and me. Blackheart Bill is forcing us to work for him and to hand over any plunder."

"*Zounds.* That's bad. You're his slaves, then."

Jon felt a cold prickle of foreboding. "We'll escape when we reach Port Royal."

The navigator shook his head. "Never. When we reach Port Royal, he'll lock you in the hold. I've heard terrible stories of pirate slaves. You'll never get away. You'll work for him until you die."

The following morning, three more ships belonging to Captain Morgan's fleet sailed out of the mist to join them.

Now they were five ships in all. Hot sun burned away the fog and burnished the ocean with gold light. The deadly fleet sailed smoothly across a glassy sea.

Fortune made a face. "I've offered to be a barrelman again."

Jon raised his eyebrows. "Why? You're scared as a cat stuck in a tree up in that crow's nest."

Fortune scratched her matted, blond hair, which she'd plaited and fastened tightly to her head with bits of string. "It's the only place I can pee in private. Can't hang off the bulwarks like our pirate friends over there."

"Makes sense." Jon laughed, avoiding the sight of the pirates sitting on the edge with their behinds hanging over the ocean. "We can't have you pooping on the poop-deck."

"Funny, aren't you?" Fortune said as Captain Morgan appeared and called the crew together.

"Gentlemen," Captain Morgan said. "I've received an interesting letter from the Governor of Jamaica, Sir

Thomas Modyford, himself." He raised a parchment covered with elegant writing. "This letter of marque authorizes me to stop Spain's attacks on England's vessels."

The pirates looked impressed.

Captain Morgan gave a small mock bow.

"I have accepted this honor on our behalf," the captain said. "It's privateers we are now. We fight the Spanish with the blessings of the King of England." He gave a lopsided grin. "Almost part of England's Royal Navy we are, me hearties."

Jon frowned. Was this true?

Cook cheered. "Me ma would be right proud of me!

Always wanted me to join England's Royal Navy, she did."

Rubbing his chin, Captain Morgan grew pensive. He lit his pipe and stared across the blue Caribbean waters. "I have in mind to try one of the vastest missions ever attempted on these seas."

Jon did not like the sound of that.

Captain Morgan blew out a cloud of smoke. "We have a fleet of fine ships and a large crew. Mark my words, I'll make us famous, men. The world will know of Captain Morgan and his band of brethren. We'll give them a story they'll never forget."

"More booty!" Rusty Pete yelled.

Captain Morgan nodded, tapped the ashes from his pipe, and tucked it into his pocket. "We set a course for the friendly island of Tortuga. We need a fleet of fellow pirates, our own buccaneer navy. In Tortuga, we'll find willing partners-in-arms, and we'll stock up on provisions."

As Captain Morgan strode away, Blackheart Bill's shadow loomed over Jon and Fortune.

Jon squinted up at him. "What's the big mission?"

Blackheart Bill sneered. "You'll see. You'd just better hope it's enough to earn a large booty. I feel the price of your freedom is rising."

The price was rising? This was exactly what Thomas had warned him about.

"He'll never let us go," Fortune whispered after Blackheart Bill strode away.

"We'll escape in Tortuga. Captain Morgan said it's a friendly island. Surely someone will help us. We'll hide until it's safe and then find working passage on a merchant ship."

The next day, Jon woke to the sound of screeching gulls. Before he could sit up, Blackheart Bill tipped his hammock, and Jon crashed to the deck.

"Wakey, wakey," Blackheart Bill yelled.

Jon blinked in the sunlight, shocked to see an emerald green island rising up out of the ocean. Tortuga—they'd arrived. They could escape!

Captain Morgan's five ships bobbed in the turquoise harbor. On the mast of each vessel, a Jolly Roger skull-and-crossbones flag waved in the breeze.

"Get to work, ye puke-faced rat," Blackheart Bill snarled. "You and your skinny mate are scraping barnacles dockside today."

Rubbing his shoulder, Jon waited for Fortune to join him. Together they sauntered down to the dock, careful not to grin at one another lest they raise Blackheart Bill's suspicions.

Morning bustle filled the quayside with noise and the smell of freshly caught fish. Weather-beaten, wooden taverns lined the harbor. Tiny houses, scruffy tents, and lean-tos nestled under palm trees, and thick jungle covered the hills. Great! They'd hide, live off the land, and beg for work on the first passing merchant ship.

Jon breathed it all in. The sweet smell of freedom.

"Zounds," Fortune gulped, elbowing him.

"What?"

"This island is teeming with pirates."

She was right. The taverns were full to bursting.

Out at sea, sails billowed on the horizon. "Look, here

come more of them. Word must have spread about Captain Morgan's big mission."

Blackheart Bill sauntered up. "Quit yer yammering and get scraping."

As they scraped barnacles from the *Satisfaction*'s hull, Jon studied the new arrivals. There were cold-eyed pirate captains in stained velvet coats. Rowdy ruffians carried pistols, swords, and cutlasses. Some hobbled on peg legs, and some gestured with hooks. They numbered in the thousands, all strolling up and down the wharf and disappearing through the dark doors of noisy watering holes.

Outside the nearest tavern, two little fair-haired boys in ragged breeches scratched for coins in the sand.

Several yards away, a furious voice roared. "Draw ye sword, ye bottom-feeding weevil!"

"I'll slice your ear off, I will," a pirate roared back.

"Fight, fight! Give him a cutlass sandwich!" a gruff voice yelled.

Cheering spectators gathered around the two burly pirates, who lunged at one another, swords clashing.

"Now's our chance," Jon said. "Follow me."

Heart thundering, Jon dropped his scraper. Pretending to be curious, he headed for the crowd with Fortune close on his heels.

They shoved their way into the crush of spectators. No one paid them any mind as they wove to the far side. Walking casually, they passed a tavern and slipped between two tents.

Then, they ran.

Up the muddy road they sprinted, past a stone fortress and into the thick jungle. Pushing through the undergrowth and scrambling over roots of sandalwood trees, they came to a large cave.

What luck!

Jon darted inside. "This is perfect. We'll hide here," he panted.

But the deeper they went, the more guarded he became.

Shadows shifted in the weak light, and he heard something moving in the back. What if they'd walked straight into a panther's den? He felt for his knife. Gone—he'd forgotten—Blackheart Bill had grabbed it.

The noise came again, a shuffling sound.

Jon opened his mouth to yell *run* when a thin, fair-haired boy emerged into the misty rays that filtered in from the cave's mouth. He looked around five years old, but he carried a long, serrated knife.

"What do you want?" the boy asked.

"We won't hurt you." Jon held out his hand.

In a flash, the boy jabbed his knife into Jon's palm. "Get out."

"Hey!" Jon leaped back and pressed his fingers to his bleeding wound. "Watch it with that knife!"

Fortune grabbed the boy's arm and shook it hard, making him drop the weapon. "Why'd you do that?"

Before he could speak, frantic footsteps sounded outside.

Jon spun to see two more fair-haired boys charging

into the cave. They were the beggars who'd been searching for coins outside the tavern.

"This is our place," the tallest shouted. He looked no older than seven, yet his blue eyes shone as cold as a pirate captain.

The smaller boy sank sharp little teeth into Fortune's arm.

Fortune shrieked and shoved him away.

"Quit it!" Jon said. "We're just looking for a place to spend the night. We'll be leaving as soon as we find a passage on a merchant ship."

The tallest boy jeered. "No merchant ships come here. Tortuga is a pirate island. You must be stupid." He drew a dagger from his waistband. "Now pay up, or I'll cut off your nose."

Jon gave the dagger a solid kick. It went flying.

The three little boys bolted out of the cave and disappeared into the jungle.

"I have a feeling they're right," Fortune said. "That's why Captain Morgan called it a friendly island. It's friendly to pirates. We'll be stuck here forever."

Jon grimaced. "We better get back to the ship. Before we're missed."

At the dockside, Cook sat smoking wild boar meat on a wooden frame over a fire. Jon was relieved when Cook waved them over. No one had noticed they'd been gone.

"This here's a *buccan*," Cook said, slipping them some tasty bites. "It's why they call us pirates *buccaneers*, m' lads."

Hungrily, Jon tucked into the salted, fatty pork rind. It was one of the best things he'd ever eaten.

Fortune said, "Hey Cook, do merchant ships ever come to Tortuga?"

Cook roared with laughter. "They wouldn't dare. Tortuga is pirate heaven."

Jon bit down hard on a piece of gristle. He spit it out, no longer hungry. So the little brats were right.

Tortuga Island grew more crowded over the next three days. Jon and Fortune joined thousands of pirates hunting and gathering fruit. When the vessels were stocked, Captain Morgan called a meeting.

"Our fleet sails tomorrow, me hearties!" he said. "To the fortress of Chagres, on the isthmus of Panama."

The pirates began talking fast and furiously.

"If we lay claim to Chagres, all of Panama is ours for the taking!"

"But they won't give it up easy, those Spaniards."

"Aye. They'll be hunkered down in the castle-fortress of San Lorenzo de Chagres."

"It's guarded well," a gray-haired pirate warned. "With thousands of scurvy Spanish rats in helmets and armored breastplates. Not like us boys here in our shirts and hats."

Jon and Fortune shared a worried glance.

Blackheart Bill laughed. "Pay him no mind. We'll be taking Spanish gold, m' lads. A few soldiers in tin hats won't stand in our way."

Captain Morgan clapped Blackheart Bill on the back. "It's the devil's own job, but someone has to do it."

"So we're going to Chagres," Jon whispered. "Not Port Royal. Talk about bad luck. We need a new plan."

"Maybe we can escape in Chagres and hide there," Fortune murmured.

Blackheart Bill bent over, grabbed them by their collars, and hauled them to face him. The tattooed serpents writhed on his muscled forearms. "What are you bilge-rats planning?"

Jon smiled widely. "Just talking about treasure."

"Uh-huh, well, you'd best hope you get me a lot of it. And if you're thinking of escaping in Chagres, forget it, the Spaniards won't help you. They hate the English. So get ready to start fighting and putting silver in me pockets."

Jon gave Blackheart Bill a mock salute.

The pirate cuffed his ear. "Count yerself lucky I don't string you up from the yardarm for insubordination. But I want you in fighting condition, now, don't I?" He patted Jon on the head. "Be good, puppy of mine."

As the crook strode away, Jon fisted his hands.

"Don't bet on it," he muttered through gritted teeth. "We're escaping as soon as our boots hit the shore, Blackheart Bill, and you'll never see us again."

He just hoped it was a promise he could keep.

10

The ocean's gulfstream bore the *Satisfaction* swiftly across the Caribbean Sea, along with a fleet of thirty pirate ships. They soon arrived at Chagres, all flying the pirate flag.

Jon stood on deck, eyeing the battlements on shore. The castle-fortress of San Lorenzo de Chagres loomed on a cliff overlooking the bay. High stone walls and iron battlements surrounded it on all sides.

He shouted in alarm as a gun fired on them from above. The warning shot boomed out over the water.

"Retreat!" the captain shouted, "Head for that bay yonder."

They anchored a league away from the fortress in a small cove.

Jon listened as the captain laid out their plan of attack. They'd hike through the jungle and come at the fort from behind. But to reach the entrance, Jon, Fortune, and the pirates faced a deadly challenge. First, they'd have to climb down a thirty-foot ravine, at the bottom of which lay a deep moat. They'd have to wade across it and scale the opposite side.

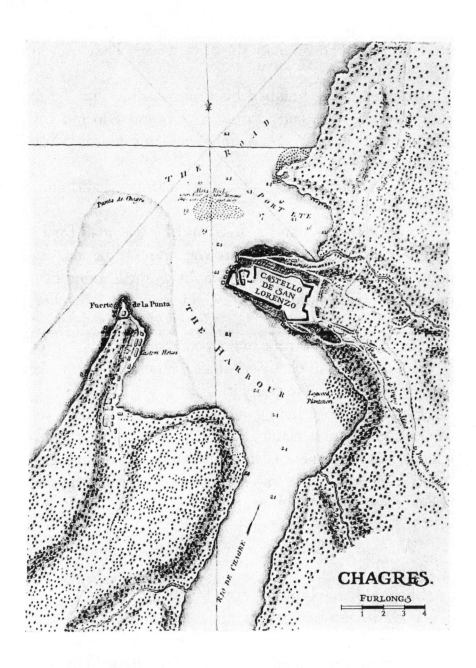

CHAGRES.

FURLONGS

Spanish soldiers would be watching them through arrow slits in the walls above. It would be easy for the soldiers to pick them off one by one.

His blood thumped in his ears. Would the captain

send him and Fortune in the first wave? They weren't trained soldiers.

Blackheart Bill grabbed his arm, startling him. "Take your weapons," he said, supplying Jon and Fortune with muskets and swords. "And fight well, my kiddies. Your freedom depends on it."

Nearby, Rusty Pete had a musket in one hand and a pistol in the other.

Jon felt trapped and scared, and he was glad for the weapons. No matter what, this was going to be a savage fight. But how long could he fight against trained, armored Spanish soldiers and live? He was just a whaler's son.

He glanced at Fortune, who looked queasy.

"I don't like our chances," she said, hefting her musket with one skinny arm to study it.

He felt a laugh rising—a sort of maniacal laugh. Just weeks ago, Pa had claimed Jon was too young to hunt whales. Now here he was, heading into a colossal battle.

"I can't wait to see Pa's face when I tell him," he said. "I bet he'll take me whaling after this."

"If you live," Fortune said darkly.

"We won't fight unless we need to. The minute we can escape, we run."

She nodded, rolling her eyes. "Obviously."

They'd been uneasy friends ever since the stew incident when Fortune had been caught. But now, suddenly, they grinned at one another, the past forgotten. They were in this together. And together, they'd escape.

For one brief moment, Jon imagined himself and Fortune hiding on board until the pirates left, then sailing away to freedom.

But they were forced to disembark in a tide of pirates. The buccaneers swarmed ashore, leaping out of rowboats.

The mob struggled through the trees and vines, surging toward the ravine that guarded the castle-fortress of San Lorenzo de Chagres. They paused when the fort came into view. It looked monstrous.

Blackheart Bill shook his fist at the battlements. "Draw yer swords, ye bottom-feeding Spanish bilge rats! We're coming for you."

Jon and Fortune, surrounded on all sides by shouting brigands, were forced over the hill's edge. They scrambled into the ravine, pressed shoulder-to-shoulder amid four hundred screaming pirates.

They splashed through the moat, the foul green water drenching Jon's face and clothes. On the far side, they scrambled up the steep, stony hillside. Rocks and gravel flew from Jon's feet. Spaniards sent musket shots raining down.

Still, Jon kept climbing, forced upward alongside dozens of sweat-soaked arms and legs.

"Did you think you'd ever be doing this?" Fortune puffed.

"No, never," Jon said. "Keep your head down."

It felt like a miracle when they reached the wall. Pirates were stuffing pots with cloth and oil. They set them alight and hurled the fireballs over the ramparts, cheering as the makeshift bombs cleared the top.

Musket shots screamed over their heads.

"Duck!" Jon shouted as enemy pots came raining down.

One exploded next to him, and he reeled at the awful smell. It wasn't a firebomb; it was a stinkpot.

"Gack, it's foul," he choked, wiping his streaming eyes with his shirt.

Fortune shook a fist at the Spaniards. "Keep ye putrid piss, ye smelly Spanish pissers."

A stinkpot flew at Jon's head. He rolled sideways, the pot narrowly missing him, and saw a gypsy-dark pirate fall to his knees.

An arrow jutted from the pirate's chest!

Jon leaped to help.

But the pirate yanked the arrow out, wrapped the tip in cotton, and set it alight. Then he used his musket to shoot it back into the fortress.

"Take this, ye pig-faced baboons!" shouted the pirate.

Wow, Jon thought. Imagine pulling an arrow out of your own chest!

The arrow sailed over the ramparts and struck a tower's thatched roof. The roof whooshed into a bright blaze that quickly spread to another tower.

Then *kaboom!*

Something exploded, shaking the whole fortress.

Jon's mouth opened in shock.

Beside him, the powder monkey jumped up and down, shouting in delight. "The fire must have spread to their barrels of gunpowder. What a lucky shot! You've blown the whole place up!"

He was right. Above the fortress, fiery sparks billowed into the air. The wood and thatch towers visible above the walls were all ablaze. Dark silhouettes of Spanish soldiers raced around. Jon guessed they were desperately trying to douse the flames.

Blackheart Bill shouted, "Forward, men! Through the gates. Victory or death! No surrender, no retreat!"

Madness filled the air. Muskets firing, four hundred savage pirates plunged into the fortress, where thick smoke whirled and flames crackled.

Jon, still on the hillside, watched as Spanish soldiers leaped over the ramparts. They were abandoning their castle!

But then the soldiers came at Jon and Fortune in their battle armor.

Fortune raised her musket in trembling hands.

"This way," Jon shouted and hauled her into the billowing smoke. Crawling, barely able to see, they scurried down the hillside.

This was it—time to make their escape.

The castle ramparts crumbled under another explosion. It was in ruins, flames burning bright. A heavy gust of wind tore away Jon's cover of smoke, and he froze in place as the pirates began to cheer.

"We've won," they cried. "We've won!"

Jon and Fortune grimaced as pirates surged around them. The press of bodies carried them along, heading at full tilt to loot the now helpless garrison.

B ack aboard, the pirates distributed the booty.
Blackheart Bill claimed Jon and Fortune's share and scoffed. "It'll take a lot more than this to pay me off, it will." Sneering, he joined the other pirates downing *Kill Devil Rum*.

Jon and Fortune watched in glum silence, aching all over from the fight.

"Well fought, gentlemen," Captain Morgan said. "And I've more good news. It's time for the second part of our mission."

Another mission, already? Jon and Fortune groaned.

"By taking Fort San Lorenzo de Chagres, we've destroyed Spain's defense on the coast. Now, we're going to take the golden City of Panama!" Captain Morgan said.

The pirates began talking in excited voices.

"Full of gold, Panama City is!" cried Rusty Pete.

Captain Morgan's lips curled and his eyes gleamed. "The Spanish will be waiting for us to attack from the sea, but we'll fool them, me hearties. We'll sail inland, up the Chagres River. Then we'll trek through the jungle, and mount a surprise attack from behind."

The pirates cheered.

Jon and Fortune groaned.

Blackheart Bill approached and clapped Jon hard on the back. "Lucky you, you're on the mission." The pirate pointed at Fortune. "You'll stay aboard and help guard our vessels."

She sneered. "Aye aye, good sir."

"Are you mocking me?" He raised his arm to cuff her.

"Careful. My parents won't pay for damaged goods."

Muttering, he wandered away.

Fortune sighed. "So much for a chance to escape in Panama City. He's only keeping me behind so that we don't take off."

Jon said, "Or because he doesn't want both his slaves to perish."

"I'm sorry you have to go," Fortune said.

Jon put on his bravest face. "I'll be all right. We just have to make it to Port Royal. But when we get there, we can't take any chances. We'll have to leap into the harbor and swim for shore."

Fortune paled. "I can't swim."

Jon rubbed his head. "Right. I forgot. Well, we'll think of something."

He hoped.

The following day, sixteen hundred pirates set off up the Chagres River in seven shallow-hulled sloops and thirty-six stolen riverboats and canoes.

Straining at the oars, Jon, Cook, and eight other pirates rowed a canoe crammed with swords, muskets, and munitions. But the river grew shallower and shallower as the tide rushed out.

"Climb out and pull," a pirate growled.

Together, they hauled the heavily laden canoe over rocks and rapids. Mud sucked at Jon's feet, and the stink of rotting foliage assaulted his nose.

After two grueling days, Captain Morgan shouted, "Abandon the boats. Load up the weapons. We travel on foot."

With his weapons wrapped in a blanket and slung over his back, Jon hacked through the jungle, choked by clouds of mosquitoes.

"My stomach thinks my throat is cut," Cook complained. "I'm starving."

"I could eat a horse," Jon agreed.

But their hunger only grew worse.

By the fourth day, four hundred pirates were too weak from fever, hunger, or injuries to travel further. Jon had no intention of dying in this bug-infested jungle. He forced himself onward.

After five miserable days, Jon and two advance guards climbed a high hill. They looked down and froze.

On the muddy plains below, thousands of Spanish foot soldiers, flanked by cavalry on prancing horses, awaited them. Helmets, muskets, lances, swords, and metal breastplates gleamed in the sunlight. Red and gold banners fluttered in the wind.

So much for the pirates' surprise attack. How had the Spanish found out?

He raced back to warn Captain Morgan. "The Spaniards are lined up and waiting—thousands of foot soldiers, hundreds of cavalry. We're outnumbered three to one. They knew. They're ready for us, sir."

"No turning back now." Captain Morgan took a leisurely draw of his pipe. "Cheer up, boy. Our men found cows and donkeys while you were gone. Cook is roasting them as we speak. Eat well, m' lad. We attack at sunrise."

Cold fear wrapped around Jon's heart. He'd survived the last attack. But how long did he have before his luck gave out?

Despite dreading the battle, he managed to devour a thick, rare-cooked steak. Stomach full at last, he slept soundly. He woke at dawn to find the pirates preparing to fight.

Captain Morgan gathered them together and gave instructions. "Gain that hill, and we shall have the advantage, me hearties. Sharpshooters, take position behind cover. We'll take Panama or die trying. No surrender, no retreat." He raised his sword. "Victory or death!"

Shouting, "Victory or death!" the pirates charged ahead.

Blackheart Bill ran behind Jon, his stinky breath puffing over him. Cook ran at his side. On the summit, they paused.

Below, Spanish cavalry stormed toward them across the plains, their lances outstretched. Cries of *"Viva el Rey!"* and the thunder of hooves filled the air.

Jon's blood throbbed in his ears.

"Wait 'till they're close." Captain Morgan shouted. He raised his clenched fist. "To victory! Fire!"

The two hundred sharpshooters—French pirates, chosen for their deadly accuracy—burst into action, picking off targets. After the first rank fired, the second rank took their place, followed by the third, firing and re-loading their muskets.

The Spaniards' horses panicked under the well-coordi-nated attack. They stumbled in the mud, bucking and whinnying.

Stunned, Jon watched most of the cavalry beat a swift retreat.

"They be running away!" Cook shouted.

The pirates raced down the hill after them, whooping in delight.

Jon felt wild relief. They'd won the battle. He'd survived.

But then the earth began to shake.

Jon couldn't believe his eyes. Driven by yelling *va-quero,* thousands of wild bulls stampeded across the field to trample the pirates. Behind the animals ran thousands of Spanish foot soldiers, driving the bulls with pikes.

The Spaniards had tricked them and lured them down from the hill!

Captain Morgan shouted, "Fire! No retreat!"

No retreat? Killed by a bull? What a horrible, stupid way to die. Trapped in the melee, with musket-fire ringing in his ears, Jon joined the men as they fired, reloaded, and fired again at the fast-approaching bulls.

It was no use. He was going to die.

But then several bulls fell, and the animals behind stumbled. They scattered and stampeded. Doubling back, they trampled the Spanish foot soldiers and charged full-tilt into what was left of the cavalry.

Horses neighed, and men screamed as the Spaniards fled.

Captain Morgan's crazy plan had worked.

"We push onward for Panama City!" Captain Morgan shouted. "Full speed ahead."

As the hordes began to move, an ear-splitting explosion rang out in the distance. Plumes of smoke rose on the horizon.

Jon stared in confusion. What was happening now?

"The Spaniards are blowing up the city," Captain Morgan roared in rage. "They're destroying our booty. If they can't have it, they don't want us to have it either. Run, men. Run!"

Trapped in the mob, Jon raced across the plains, down a cobbled road, and into Panama City.

The fire burned bright, staining the sky orange. The cathedral's tall steeples, the stately churches, and the beautifully tiled mansions were all aflame.

Pirates raced from house to house, from church to cathedral, grabbing what treasures they could, howling, plundering, drinking, gorging themselves on food.

The sight of the burning city and frantic people was terrible. Jon found a bucket, and together with his old sailing-mates from the *Princess*, they tried to put out the fires.

"Forget the fire. Grab the gold," Cook yelled.

"And rob the citizens." Rusty Pete gave a wild laugh. "Find out where they've hidden their goods. Ye may have to tickle them with ye cutlass."

The flames wouldn't be quenched. Jon could only gulp in despair at what they'd done.

Captain Morgan declared it time to return to the Chagres River mouth.

"Nice takings," Rusty Pete said, strapping a sack on a mule. "Two hundred mules loaded with plunder. Look at this! A gold chalice and a jeweled crucifix. Silk dresses. These look like the Governor's wife's pearls. And a huge lot of prisoners too."

Jon stared. "We're taking prisoners back through the jungle to the ship?"

"Ransom, lad. Ransom." Cook shook his head and roared with laughter. "Ye have a lot to learn."

Captain Morgan's army arrived at the Chagres River mouth in a triumphant mood. Unfortunately, they were met with terrible news.

Fortune ran to meet Jon, eyes wide with fear.

"What happened?" Jon asked.

"Last night, the *Satisfaction* sank. And four ships with her. A storm blew them onto a reef."

Jon stared at her. "The *Satisfaction* sank?"

"Yes. If Captain Morgan finds out I'm a girl, he'll blame me." Fortune was shaking. "He'll keelhaul us both."

Jon gulped. What if Blackheart Bill revealed their secret?

Captain Morgan rounded everyone up. "The victory is still ours. I will take command of the sloop, the *Fury*. Some of you will join me, and others will be divided amongst the remaining ships. Now load up the treasure."

Rusty Pete stepped forward. "All of you mates who plundered Panama City, you'll strip before boarding—we gotta make sure you handed over all your booty. Don't want anyone hidin' nothing."

Good thing Fortune doesn't have to strip, Jon thought, or it would be over.

After the plunder was distributed between the thirty pirate captains, men were assigned to ships, and the fleet sailed away.

Jon thought of all who'd lost their lives for gold—on both sides of the battle. He could still picture the burning town and the people who'd lost their homes and knew he never wanted to be a pirate.

"You'll be mighty pleased with your share of the plunder," Captain Morgan told his crew. "I'll keep it safe in my treasure chests. We'll divide it up when we reach Port Royal."

"We won't get any," Fortune muttered. "It's terrible to be a slave."

"We'll escape in Port Royal," Jon said. "Or die trying."

"Forget that victory or death stuff," Fortune muttered. "It doesn't work for me."

Blackheart Bill loomed over them. "You're a curse to us all, little lady," he whispered, glaring at Fortune. "The ransom is now 150,000 silver coins each."

Fortune's eyes filled with tears. She dashed them away.

J on stood at the *Fury's* bulwark and watched with relief as the green mountains of Jamaica finally appeared on the horizon.

"I'll be mighty happy to see Port Royal," Rusty Pete said. "There'll be rum flowing down the streets and pretty girls aplenty."

"Aye! Port Royal." Blackheart Bill rattled the coins in his pockets, including those he'd seized from Jon and Fortune. "I've got plenty to spend." He shot Jon and Fortune a shark-like grin. "And more coming."

"Revenge would be sweet," Fortune muttered.

"Freedom would be sweeter." Jon studied Port Royal's harbor. Houses painted candy-pink and mint-green dotted terraced hills. A round tower and massive fortress protected the city.

"Looks a nice place," he said.

"It's not bad." Fortune scratched her matted hair. "I told you. I was born here." She squashed a louse between two fingers. "At Rosewood Hall plantation."

Jon began to feel optimistic. "You said your stepfather's mean, but surely your mother will help you?"

"No."

"She's your mother! She has to help," Jon said.

"Tell her that." Fortune rubbed her eyes, and Jon saw she'd chewed her nails raw. "But if we can get ashore, I think I know where to find help."

Jon looked at the turquoise harbor. If only Fortune could swim! They could slip overboard and escape to freedom. But that wasn't possible. They'd have to disembark with the others.

As the vessel came to anchor, pirates jostled, all eager

to go ashore. Nerves hopping, Jon lined up behind Fortune, keeping a watch for Blackheart Bill.

"When we reach the wharf, get ready to run," Jon whispered.

Without warning, steely fingers sank into his arm. "You two are coming to the hold," Blackheart Bill snarled.

"We're not," Jon said. "We're getting off in Port Royal."

"Dream on, ye thumb-sucking snot rags," Blackheart Bill snarled. "I'll deliver my demands to your parents. You'll wait in the hold until I have the ransom in me pockets."

"That's not fair!" Fortune's cheeks went pink with fury.

Throwing back his head, Blackheart Bill laughed. "Pirates are never fair. Surely ye know that by now, ye sniveling little rat poop."

Cook let out a shout. "The Royal Navy's come to meet us and honor us, m' lads."

Jon spun to see an official-looking vessel tying up alongside the *Fury*.

Three military officers in Royal Navy uniforms boarded the ship. Jon felt dizzy with relief. This was the best thing he'd ever seen. Suddenly, unbelievably, they were saved!

"Officer! Sir!" he shouted.

A knifepoint poked his ribs. He froze.

"Another peep and you're fish food," Blackheart Bill growled.

An officer with a hawk-like nose said, "Who is the captain of this ship?"

Captain Morgan stepped forward. He wore a hat adorned with a huge feather.

Bowing, he smiled. "Greetings. How are you, Lieutenant Grantley?"

"Identify yourself, sir," the lieutenant said.

Captain Morgan frowned. "You know who I am, Grantley! I'm Captain Henry Morgan."

Lieutenant Grantley cleared his throat. "It is my duty, Henry Morgan, to place you under arrest on a charge of piracy."

Jon shot Fortune a look.

"That's ridiculous!" Captain Morgan said.

"By the authority of Charles II, King of England, it is my duty to arrest you," Lieutenant Grantley said. "And by order of Governor Sir Thomas Modyford."

"On what charge?" Captain Morgan demanded.

"It's been brought to the Governor's attention that you attacked and plundered the Spanish city of Panama."

"I sailed to Panama with the full knowledge of Jamaica's Governor. King Charles II himself approved of our actions," Captain Morgan said. "I carry a letter of marque from Governor Modyford. I am a privateer, not a pirate. The letter of marque authorizes me to attack England's enemies. Spain is an enemy nation."

"Not anymore, sir."

"What in the devil's name do you mean?" Captain Morgan said.

"It seems, sir, that the news has not yet reached you," Lieutenant Grantley said. "A peace treaty has been signed between England and Spain."

"Whoops," Fortune whispered.

"Many pirates are already in jail," Lieutenant Grantley continued. "Taylor was hung last week."

"Taylor!" Captain Morgan cried. "Hung?"

Jon knew he had to speak up, or they'd be imprisoned along with the pirates. "I'm not a pirate!" he shouted. "I'm a prisoner."

But the officials ignored him, and Blackheart Bill's knife pressed harder.

Captain Morgan glared at the lieutenant. "My crew and I are not pirates. We are privateers."

Lieutenant Grantley's face was grim. "Unfortunately, sir, Taylor was under that assumption as well. Now he's dead. Baker will hang tomorrow."

"Baker? He operates with the blessings of the Governor himself," Captain Morgan said.

"No longer. Soon he will operate hanging from a

gibbet in High Street Square. And you all will join him shortly."

Captain Morgan went red with anger.

Jon's heart thundered. How could he and Fortune prove they weren't pirates? Nobody would believe them.

And the punishment for piracy was hanging!

R ed-coated guards marched Jon, Fortune, and the
pirates down a cobbled street filled with taverns.

On High Street, they passed the gallows, a low cross-
beam with a thick dangling rope. The hangman's noose
swung in the breeze.

Jon couldn't look.

Townspeople pointed and jeered at them. A woman
with crimson lips pulled at his canvas shirt and laughed.

"You'll look mighty good, swinging from a rope, love,"
she called.

"A short drop, and a sudden stop," a man hollered,

Jon turned to a guard and tried to explain that he and
Fortune weren't pirates.

The guard chuckled. "Tell that to your cellmates."

The prisoners were led into a bleak stone building. Inside, hollow-eyed prisoners stared out between thick bars.
Some shook the bars and yelled.

Jon, Fortune, Cook, and Rusty Pete were shoved into a
cramped cell.

Fortune looked around and winced. "No beds. Just a

jar of water, a bucket that stinks of pee, and rat poop all over."

The guard gave her a sarcastic laugh. "Don't worry, you won't be here long. You'll be hanging in the fresh air real soon." He slammed and locked the cell door.

Jon called after him. "Sir, when will our trial be?"

"Tomorrow."

"Tomorrow?" Cook moaned, looking sick with fear. "We're dead men walking, me hearties."

Rusty Pete scowled. "We'll swing and sun-dry by the week's end if we don't do something fast."

Fortune bent double and retched—whether from the stink or from terror, Jon couldn't say.

She wiped her mouth. "We've got to get out of here!"

"I'm working on it." Jon stared through the small, high window at the sky.

He tried to come up with a plan, but his mind spun with images:

Wooden steps leading up to the platform.

The dangling rope.

The hangman's noose.

He couldn't think—couldn't control the fear roiling through him. They'd come so close to escaping. Now it was all over.

Cook and Rusty Pete waited with bated breath to hear Jon's plan. Black despair washed over him.

Finally, he sighed, "I've got nothing."

"I have an idea," Fortune said.

Rusty Pete heaved a sigh of relief. "Good lad!"

Jon moved closer. "Tell us."

Huddled together, they listened to Fortune's idea.

"It's risky," Jon said. "No one assaults a guard and

lives. And we'll ruin any chance to prove we're not pirates."

Rusty Pete gave a dry laugh. "Every man in this jail is claimin' he's not a pirate, m' lad."

Jon nodded. "All right. Let's try it."

"Lend me your shirt, Jon," Fortune said.

He handed it over. She tied the sleeves around her waist, fastening the knot at the back. At the front, the shirt hung down to her ankles. In the dim light, it passed for a long skirt. Undoing her braids, she finger-combed her matted, blond hair. Quickly, she washed her face with water from the jar.

"What you think?" she asked.

"You almost look like a girl!" Cook said, squinting at her. "Well done, m' lad! The guard will throw a fit when he sees you. He'll be in big trouble for lockin' up a girl in here."

"Good!" Fortune said. "That means he'll unlock the cell door to get me out."

Jon spoke up. "Rusty Pete, you're the biggest. Get ready to hit him with the pee bucket."

"Good plan," Rusty Pete said. "But we best wait until they change guards. The one who locked us up might not fall for it, seeing as none of us was girls when he stuck us in here."

With tense faces, the four sat waiting. After what seemed hours, Jon heard the new guard's heavy boots thump along the corridor as he began his rounds.

They all snapped upright.

Fortune looked at Jon. "Remember, we're pretending you're my brother."

"I haven't forgotten." Despite the suffocating heat, he

felt cold.

"Here goes." Fortune called out in a high, sweet voice, "Excuse me! Help? Can someone help me?"

The guard, a young man with a wispy beard, rushed toward her.

Fortune said, "Kind sir. It's time for me to go home."

"A girl?" the guard stammered. "Girls can't be in here! You'll get me into terrible trouble, miss. What're you doing in here?"

"I was saying a prayer with my dearest brother." Fortune's voice trembled. "We've said our prayers and our goodbyes now, sir."

"How did you get in?" The guard gaped, stunned. "Who are you?"

"I'm Lady Florabelle Rosewood, sir. I'm the daughter of Lady Cecilia Rosewood and the late Lord James Rosewood of Rosewood Hall. My step-father is Colonel Montgomery."

"Rosewood! Lady Florabelle Rosewood?" the guard stammered. "Oh my goodness! It's not safe for you in here, milady. These are pirates. Ruthless men! I can't imagine who allowed you in here."

"It was the kind guard before you." Fortune wiped a tear from her eye. "I begged him to let me say a prayer for my brother's immortal soul." She gave a soft sob. "It was a sad, sad day for my family when my brother left the plantation and went to sea. He's an innocent boy, sir, and soon he will be hung." She began to sob, big loud choking sobs.

Despite his fears, Jon almost snorted with laughter.

"The guard never should have done that! Never!" the man cried. "Lady Florabelle, I'm deeply sorry for your problems, but you must leave immediately." He took a bunch of keys from his belt.

Jon watched, barely breathing.

"My poor brother!" Fortune put her head in her hands and blubbered in earnest as the guard unlocked the door.

"I'm so sorry," the guard said. "You have to leave, milady." He took a few steps into the cell and touched her arm.

Rusty Pete leaped from the shadows and whacked him over the head with the pee bucket.

The guard went down like a log.

"Oh dear," Fortune said. "I feel mean. He was nice. Let's get out of here."

"Tie him up," Jon said. "Quick, gag him with your scarf."

As they bound and gagged the guard, Fortune tore off her fake skirt, tossed it to Jon, and rewound her hair up into a knot. Together, the four dashed out into the hall.

The other pirates, who'd heard the commotion, stood at their bars hissing, "Get us out of here!"

The powder monkey reached out a thin arm. "The keys, Jon! Don't let me hang. Help us, mate!"

Jon pressed the keys into the powder monkey's hand.

"Good lad!" Captain Morgan cried.

Sticking to the shadows, Jon and Fortune—followed by a seething mass of pirates—ran through the dark jailhouse, out the prison gates, and down the winding side streets of Port Royal.

Ducking into an alley, Jon pulled Fortune behind a pile of reeking crates. They stood catching their breath.

"I'll protect you, fair maiden," Jon said. "That was great."

"Don't make me punch you," Fortune panted.

"If Blackheart Bill got out of jail with the others, he'll be after us," Jon said.

"Let's borrow a boat, row to the *Fury*, and grab our share of the plunder," Fortune said. "Then we'll buy a passage on the next ship out of here." She fastened her hair more tightly, securing it at the nape of her neck. "There. Now I'm Fortune again. It was awful being Florabelle. I never could stand that name." She peered around. "I'm sorry to say, I've no idea where we are."

"If we keep running downhill," Jon said. "We're bound to get to the wharf. Hurry, the jail guards will be hunting us down. And Blackheart Bill could show up at any moment."

More than once, Jon and Fortune had to hide and wait for prison guards to pass.

When they finally reached the harbor, it was dark and quiet.

Gasping, Fortune pointed out to sea. "That looks like the *Fury*! And she's leaving Port Royal."

The *Fury's* familiar sails shimmered in the moonlight as the sloop sailed out of the harbor.

"What the heck?" Fortune cried. "There goes our treasure."

"Where are they going? Not out to sea. It looks like they're turning to follow the coast."

Jon heard footsteps. He pulled Fortune into the shadows.

Cook ran up and gaped at the departing ship. "They're stealing my plunder! I busted me fat gut for me share!" he puffed. "Those scurvy dogs won't get away with this." He ran to a jollyboat, which was tied to the dock.

Fortune shot out of their hiding spot. "Wait for us!"

"What are you doing?" Jon cried.

"They'll hang us if we stay in Port Royal," she said.

71

"Good point."

They ran to join Cook. Using three sets of oars, they pulled furiously through the dark ocean in pursuit of the swift sailing *Fury*.

After hours, exhausted, their oars moving clumsily in the rowlocks, they rounded the island's far point.

"We'll never catch her," Cook groaned.

Fortune pointed to a partially hidden inlet. "Look! There she is."

The pirate sloop bobbed at anchor. It looked abandoned—where were all the pirates?

Cautiously, the three rowed ashore and hauled the jollyboat into a clump of beach grass.

Jon scanned the moonlit island. In the distance, two men were struggling to haul something across the sand dunes.

"They've got a sea-chest, and it looks real heavy," Jon whispered.

Cook gripped Jon's shoulder. "They're buryin' me treasure, the scurvy dogs."

"Who are they?" Fortune whispered.

"Hard to say." Jon pointed. "Look, one is short, and the other is real tall."

The men paused, then lifted the sea-chest again, and shuffled through the sand until they reached two criss-crossed palm trees.

"Let's sneak closer," Jon said.

They crawled up a vine-covered sand dune and peered over the top. The tall pirate straightened and wiped his brow.

Jon stiffened. "It's Blackheart Bill."

"Aye," Cook said. "The rat."

"I bet that's the treasure from Panama," Fortune hissed.

Jon pressed a finger to his lips.

Blackheart Bill began whittling branches into wooden pegs. His short, burly partner started digging a hole.

Everything was peaceful; the only sound the thumping shovel.

Finally, the digging stopped, the pirates lowered the chest into the ground, and the short one began filling in the hole. Meanwhile, Blackheart Bill paced the dunes in slow, measured steps. As he walked, he counted out his strides.

"One, two, three, four . . ."

At intervals, Blackheart Bill drove his wooden pegs into the sand. Each time, he marked a notation on a parchment paper. Then he paced the section again: from the crisscrossed palm trees to the shore, to a rocky outcrop and back. He checked each distance twice.

"A treasure map," Fortune said. "He's making a treasure map."

Blackheart Bill looked up, straight at them.

Jon ducked and pulled Fortune down. "Shh!"

"Did he see us?" Cook whispered.

"Don't know." Heart pounding, Jon lay as still as he could.

From beyond came thumps and an occasional clunk. He peeked again.

The two pirates were marching away across the sand toward the ship. Blackheart Bill, carrying the shovel over his shoulder, was leading. The short pirate trailed behind.

They'd gone about halfway when Blackheart Bill stopped and bent to fiddle with his boot.

The short pirate strode past him.

Suddenly, shockingly, the massive pirate rose to his full seven-foot height. Silent as a panther, he took two long steps—right up to the short pirate's back and raised the shovel.

Moonlight caught the metal as it descended.

The short pirate crashed to the sand like a downed tree.

Jon stared aghast. He couldn't believe what he'd seen.

Fortune put her hands over her eyes. "No!" she whispered. "Oh no."

Crouching, Blackheart Bill checked the pirate's wrist for a pulse. Quickly, he covered him with sand. Then, whistling, he continued walking, rhythmically swinging the shovel.

"It's a bloody murder we've seen, and we've seen too much!" Cook gasped. "If he finds out we saw, we're as dead as drowned bilge rats."

Jon nodded, swallowing hard.

When Blackheart Bill was out of sight, they ran for the rowboat. Panting, they dragged it further into the dark jungle, hiding their presence as best they could.

"He killed him!" Fortune cried.

"Aye. To keep the treasure hidden for himself. Dead men tell no tales." Cook shook his curly head sadly.

Jon felt sick. "What happened to the Pirates' Code? I thought pirates were loyal to each other."

Cook gave a hollow laugh. "It's a hard life, m' lad."

What were they to do? They couldn't go back to Port Royal. And it seemed their worst enemy was now in charge of *the Fury*.

What had happened to the other pirates?

One thing was certain.

They had to steer clear of Blackheart Bill.

I n the jungle, the night seemed to last forever. Tree frogs whistled. Mosquitoes buzzed and stung. When morning streaks of pink painted the sky, Jon climbed atop a dune.

The *Fury* had sailed.

He heaved a sigh of relief and ran to wake the others.

"Blackheart Bill's gone," he said.

"But for how long? He'll be back for his treasure," Fortune said.

"True." Jon looked thoughtful. "It would be a sorry shame if someone else dug it up. A person could use that treasure to pay for passage to somewhere safe. In my case, back home to Ma and Pa."

"Aye!" Cook beamed widely. "Digging it up works for me!"

"Me, too," Fortune cried.

Across the dunes they ran.

They reached the mound beneath the crisscrossed palm trees and began furiously digging—hand after hand, scoop after scoop.

Sweat soaked Jon's back. He was puffing for breath when his fingers hit something hard.

Zounds! The treasure chest!

His heart galloped.

He stopped and scanned the beach. Was anyone watching? His spine prickled at the thought of Blackheart Bill's spade. He remembered the pirate buried nearby.

Slowly, he said, "This treasure came from bloodshed. Maybe we shouldn't touch it."

Cook widened his eyes, the whites showing. "Are you sayin' it's bad luck? Cursed?"

Fortune shook her head. "It may be cursed for Blackheart Bill. But it's a blessing for us. It's our way out of here."

Cook crossed himself. "Saint Nicholas, patron saint of pirates, sailors, and thieves, protect us." He scrambled into the hole, bracing arms under the chest. "Heave ho!"

Muscles straining, they hauled it up. Jon smashed the padlock with a rock. Then, slowly, he raised the lid. Empty canvas sacks covered whatever lay beneath. He lifted the sacks and gasped.

"It's full to the brim!" Fortune stammered. "Oh my word. Look at the coins! Silver pieces of eight, doubloons, and guineas. English, French, and Spanish coins!"

"Ooh-hoo!" Cook shouted, laughing wildly. "Praise be to St. Nicholas!" He grabbed a sack and filled it with a stream of twinkling silver coins. "I'm rich!"

Dizzy with delight, Fortune ran her fingers through bewitching green, red, and crystal jewels, turquoise necklaces, diamond bracelets, pearls, and golden rings. "So beautiful!"

"Look at these." Jon's voice was deep with awe as he

sifted through exotic Oriental coins. "They're gold and stamped like spider webs. And these are round and square. They're bored through the center. You could wear them on a chain around your neck."

Cook paused. "We're dead men if Blackheart Bill finds out we have the treasure." His voice shook. "We must swear in blood to keep this secret."

Faces tense, they used a palm frond to poke their pointer fingers. Together, they knelt in the sand, repeating after Cook.

"I swear on my blood, and on my life, that through hell's fire or dark terrors, and no matter what befalls me, I shall not break this oath of secrecy."

There was a moment of solemn silence.

Jon said. "We should only take our share and leave the rest for the others."

"What others?" Cook said. "Only Blackheart Bill knows where the chest is buried, and he murdered one of me mates. You going to leave some for him?"

Jon followed Cook's lead, grabbing a sack and filling it to the brim with coins and jewels. Fortune did the same and crammed doubloons and gems into her pockets.

"In for a penny, in for a pound," Cook said, taking off his jackboots and filling them too. "A short life, but a merry one!"

Jon took off his socks and filled them.

The chest was still more than three-quarters full when they closed the lid.

"If Blackheart Bill returns for the booty, he'll be out for revenge," Jon said. "The sooner we leave this island, the better."

"Let's head for Port Royal," Fortune said. "We'll hide out in a warehouse until it's safe to buy our passage out of here."

Buzzing with excitement, they began the long journey back to the harbor. The three took turns rowing. It was late afternoon when they finally returned the rowboat.

Feeling exposed with his socks and bags of coins, Jon led the way, ducking into the shadows of warehouses.

"Let's try to find an unlocked shed to hide in," he whispered. "Hopefully, we can leave by tomorrow."

"Look at us!" Fortune said. "No one will sell us passage on a ship. We're filthy. We look like pirates."

A raucous yell rang out from the tavern at the wharf. "Free rum for the workers!"

"I've a terrible thirst!" Cook said.

Before Jon could stop him, Cook disappeared through a swinging tavern door. Within seconds, he came tearing back. His treasure-filled boots fell from his arms, sending coins flying everywhere.

"Blackheart Bill's in there," Cook gasped. "He saw me! Run!"

Cook fled up the cobbled street.

In horror, Jon saw Blackheart Bill's seven-foot-tall figure, his beard hanging like a hairy curtain, come charging out of the tavern.

"Follow me." Fortune tripped over a fish head, and coins flew from her pockets. She scrambled to her feet. "Run!"

Frantic to get away, Jon charged after Fortune, down winding muddy streets to the harbor. But the treasure was weighing Jon down. He made an awful decision—he dropped it and ran like the wind, powered by sheer terror.

Past boat sheds and warehouses. Along a muddy path that wound around the base of the rocky bluff. Through shallow water.

Jon's feet slipped, and he landed on his butt. He jumped up. There was no sign of Fortune. He looked around desperately. Then he heard her voice.

"Hurry. Behind the rocks."

He scrambled over a pile of stones. Fortune was crouched in the narrow entrance to a hidden cave.

"Hurry!" she said.

"Into a cave? We'll be stuck. If Blackheart Bill sees it, we'll be sitting ducks."

"It's a tunnel. Hurry, follow me." She took off like an arrow.

Jon ran.

The narrow tunnel sloped uphill, leading miles into the mountain. Smothered in pitch dark, he kept one hand on the damp stone and hoped he wouldn't collide with something or someone.

"Where are we going?"

"To my home, to Rosewood Hall."

"This tunnel leads to your home?"

"Yes. It's an escape tunnel." Fortune paused to take a breath. "It leads to the hurricane shelter. We can hide there tonight. My nanny will help us."

"Your *mommy* will help us?" Jon asked.

"No, not my mommy," Fortune said with a laugh. "My *nanny*. Nanny Quassy. She's much nicer than my mother. And miles nicer than my stepfather."

"Surely your parents will help when they hear you're in danger."

"My parents don't even want me. They never did. They wanted a son, not a daughter. Only a male can inherit Rosewood Hall."

"Oh." Jon thought Fortune's parents sounded worse by the minute. "Well, it's good your nanny will help."

"Keep going," Fortune said. "Only a few miles, and we'll be there. My nanny will help us, but we have to make sure no one else sees us." Her footsteps echoed as she took off again.

Jon began running, but his foot hit something hard. He landed flat on his face, his leg twisted under him.

He forced himself up and limped on.

A stone stairway led to a round iron grate. Jon helped Fortune shove it open. Together they crawled out into a large cement room lined with wooden boxes.

"This is the hurricane shelter," Fortune whispered. "Come on."

She pushed open the thick wooden door, and Jon peered out.

Atop a sloping hill, a palatial three-story mansion glowed ghostly white in the moonlight. Lawns and terraced gardens carpeted the hillside beneath it.

"Rosewood Hall," Fortune whispered.

"Whoa!" he said. "You really lived here?"

"Yes. Be very quiet." Fortune shot him a look. "What happened to your face?"

"Nothing." He dashed blood out of his eyes.

"Come on." Fortune led them down a winding stone path. "My nanny lives at the slave allotment."

Jon limped after her, hurrying past dancing fountains and terraced beds of sweet-smelling flowers; through a coconut grove, its tall trunks stretching for the stars.

On the far side, thatched-roof huts nestled under large breadfruit trees. Jon marveled at the view of rolling hills covered with rustling crops. It stretched as far as he could see.

"Sugarcane," Fortune whispered.

Of course, he thought, the white gold that made plantation owners rich. Fortune's family sure had a lot of it.

She pointed at the huts. "This is the slave allotment. Stay quiet. If the Overseer catches us, we'll be in big trouble. He's a brute."

He nodded, and they crept toward a hut.

Fortune tapped at the door. Nothing happened. She bit her lip, glanced at Jon, and tapped again.

Movement sounded, and the door flew open. A dark-skinned woman in a red embroidered shawl peeked out. Her eyes widened. "Miss Florabelle! Is that you?"

"Yes." Fortune rushed into her arms. "Nanny!"

They hugged until Jon cleared his throat, worried the Overseer would show up.

"Come in, quickly. Both of you," Nanny Quassy said. Inside, she lit a lamp. "Oh child, you do look a mess. Where have you been? I've been so worried."

"I wanted to tell you I was running away, but . . ."

"Never mind that now. Who is this boy with you?"

"This is my good friend, Jon," Fortune said.

"He's hurt," she said.

"It's nothing," Jon said, pressing his shirtsleeve to his forehead.

"We're in terrible trouble," Fortune said. "An evil pirate's chasing us."

"A pirate?" Nanny Quassy cried. "Well now, I'm sure that can't be true. A pirate?"

"It is true," Fortune said. "I'm sorry, I don't want to get you in trouble. We just need to hide out tonight. Tomorrow, we'll be gone. We're going to buy passage on a boat out of Port Royal in the morning."

John thought of his lost gold. He wasn't sure how they'd buy passage now; hopefully, Fortune still had enough.

"Oh, my dear Lord." Nanny Quassy opened the door, peered out as if expecting to see a horde of bandits, and shut it again. "Well, I'm sure I don't know what to think. But I'll find a bandage for Jon here. And I'm guessing you must be hungry." She looked at their dirty faces and muddy feet. "Let's get you two cleaned up."

Self-conscious, Jon removed his shoes and gave his armpit a sniff. Yikes. He felt a wreck, and his twisted leg ached. He needed to pull himself together if he was going to escape Blackheart Bill.

Nanny Quassy brought out a basin of water. While they washed, she set a plate of spicy jerk pork and bananas on the table. After she'd bandaged his head, they dug in. The food was delicious.

Jon licked his lips. "Sure tastes good, Nanny Quassy."

"Thank you, Jon." She paused. "Surely we must tell your mother you are here, Miss Florabelle?"

Fortune glanced up in fright. "No! Please, don't."

Nanny Quassy sighed. "Well, now that's your choice, I suppose."

"Do you mind if we rest here until morning?" Fortune asked.

"I'll find you some blankets," Nanny Quassy said.

Jon was grateful for a few hours of sleep. His muscles ached from digging and rowing, his ankle throbbed, and his head hurt from where he'd smacked it.

She woke them at dawn. "I think it best I go to the laundry and bring you some clean clothes. You'll never get onto a ship in those rags."

"Oh, thank you, Nanny," Fortune said.

"Stay inside, now, while I'm gone," Nanny Quassy warned.

Jon and Fortune nodded.

But as Nanny Quassy turned to leave, a loud pounding sounded at the door.

A horrible realization flashed through Jon's mind—Fortune had told Blackheart Bill where her family lived. She told him she was from Rosewood Hall. They'd been absolutely crazy to hide here.

"He's found us!" Jon whispered.

Heart thundering, he grabbed a knife. Fortune did the same. Nanny Quassy pressed her hand to her mouth.

The pounding came again.

"Oh, Nanny, I'm sorry!" Fortune whispered.

"Shh," Jon said as they all backed into the furthest corner. "We need to hide."

But where?

A loud thud—someone's boot slammed against the wood.

Bam! Another monstrous thud.

Then, the door flew open.

A fat man stood in the doorway. He wore a grey suit and held a whip in one hand.

Fortune gasped. *"The Overseer."*

Jon hastily lowered the knife.

"Good morning, Mr. Sweeny," Fortune said, her voice shaky.

"I heard we had trespassers on the property." His mouth puckered in disapproval as he eyed Fortune's ragged appearance. "Wasn't expecting you, Lady Florabelle."

Fortune raised her chin. "Will you please let my parents know I'm visiting Nanny and will be up at the Hall shortly?"

The Overseer gave Jon a hard, quizzical look. "The Colonel is on his way down here, Lady Florabelle.

Jon felt all hope for a quick escape vanish. He had a pounding desire to make a run for it.

Too late.

A stout man in a fancy blue taffeta suit thrust his way through the door. His face shook like thunder, and his eyes flashed in the lamplight. A uniformed security guard and four dark-skinned slaves followed him inside.

Fortune paled but crossed her arms. "Good morning, sir. How nice to see you."

"Nice to see me, is it?" her stepfather said. "You have a lot of explaining to do, Missy. Look at you. What a mess! And what is this you've brought with you?"

"My friend, sir," Fortune said.

"Friend indeed." Stepping closer, her stepfather prodded Jon's chest with a bamboo cane. "I saw this here boy being marched into prison just yesterday. A friend? An escaped prisoner, he is. A pirate!"

Fists clenched, Jon said, "I'm an honest seaman from the trading ship, the *Princess*. My ship was captured by pirates."

"Liar!"

"It's the truth," Fortune said. "He's not a pirate, sir. That's ridiculous."

"Ridiculous?" Her stepfather turned bright red. He spoke to the security guard. "Escort *Lady* Florabelle to her mother. And inform Lady Rosewood I will be there shortly to deal with this mess."

"Yes, sir." The security guard bowed and reached for Fortune.

"Don't you dare touch me. I will see my mother without your assistance." Fortune stalked off.

The security guard hurried after her.

Nanny Quassy wrung her hands, and Jon gave a silent groan.

Now what? We should have had a back-up plan!

Fortune's stepfather was a colonel and had the power

to throw him back in jail. He pictured the hangman's noose.

They'd been so close to escaping.

Jon had a sudden longing for his mother's kitchen and the sound of her singing. With a terrible ache, he missed their dog, Tucker. It hurt to think of his father's last, fierce hug. Why hadn't Jon listened to him? Why had he left without saying goodbye?

For the rest of their lives, his parents would search for him at the docks, wondering why he never came home.

The men pushed him outside.

An orange sun glowed on the horizon. The hill sloped down to a sweeping view of Port Royal and the sparkling blue ocean. Sailing slowly into the harbor came a beautiful merchant ship with gilded red bulwarks. England's Union Jack flag waved from her mast.

How he wished he were safely aboard.

"Thinking of going down there, are we?" The Overseer grabbed Jon and slammed him into the wall, knocking the breath out of him.

"Let go of me," Jon gasped.

Holding him by the hair, the Overseer said, "Colonel Montgomery, we could use this one as convict labor. We need strong workers for the boiling house. Our useless slaves keep dying on us. This one's healthy, well-muscled." He pinched Jon's cheek. "Open your mouth, boy. Show me your teeth."

A tide of rage rose from Jon's stomach. He had a strong urge to bite. "I'm a seaman from the *Princess*, an English merchant ship," he said loudly. Both his head and his leg throbbed violently. "Not a pirate."

"Ha!" Colonel Montgomery said, "I saw you yesterday with your hands cuffed behind your back. An escaped pirate, that's what you are. And the penalty for piracy is the hangman's noose. But I think we can fit you in around here, save your neck for better things."

He motioned to a dreadlocked slave, who stood watching with interest. "You, there. Give this pirate thirteen lashes."

The dreadlocked slave took hold of Jon. But before he could raise his whip, a sound like rolling thunder shook the air.

The small group outside Nanny Quassy's hut froze.
The noise had come from the harbor. Jon knew
that sound: cannon fire. But who was firing a cannon?

Everyone stared at the English merchant ship. Black
smoke billowed around its bow. As the smoke cleared, Jon
saw that its cannons were aimed at Port Royal!

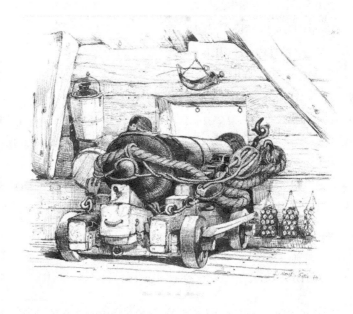

What the heck? Why would an English merchant ship fire on its own people?

A second cannon blast boomed. Then a third.

At the exact moment, England's flag came down from the mast, and Spain's flag rose in its place.

Jon understood. It had been a trick.

"Spaniards!" the Colonel shouted. "Why are they attacking us? England signed a peace treaty with Spain!"

Jon's brain whirled. Another flag rose alongside the Spanish one. This one was red with a skull and two cutlasses.

"Spanish pirates!" the Overseer shouted. "And the blood-red flag means they give no quarter. They mean to kill the lot of us."

Drums beat a frantic alarm. A trumpet sounded. Crowds ran out onto the city streets below. More pirate ships were sailing into the harbor.

"Look, the pirate's longboats are already landing on the wharf," the Colonel spluttered. "Why isn't someone doing something? Where are our warships?"

Excitement fizzed in Jon's veins. Port Royal was erupting into pandemonium. Could he take advantage of this to get away?

Two gatehouse guards raced up the path. "Colonel! We're under attack, sir!"

The Colonel's fat face went purple. "Zookers. Alert Lady Rosewood and the staff. Have the house-guards lock and barricade everything. Saddle the horses. I must get to the fort."

Panic-stricken slaves and convict workers streamed from the huts and the fields.

"Slaves! Hide in the woods," the Colonel yelled. "Stay

there until we've gutted the Spanish swine!" He jabbed the dreadlocked slave with his cane. "Ayuba! Take this pirate to the stocks. I'll deal with him later."

Ayuba nodded, but his eyes were guarded.

Mounted on horseback, the Colonel and the guards galloped down the hill.

Below, Spanish pirates were advancing steadily, driving the frantic citizens back. The rattle of musket fire filled the air. Cannonballs continued to pound the massive fort's wall, turning it to rubble.

The slaves and the convict workers watched, mesmerized. Ayuba seemed in no hurry to take Jon to the stocks. Maybe he didn't like being poked with the Colonel's cane.

Maybe he would be an ally.

Not only were Ayuba's eyes bright and intelligent, but he also possessed the bulging muscles you might get from crewing on a sailing ship. Was it possible he'd sailed before?

Taking a chance, Jon spoke in a low voice. "Ayuba, I know a ship that's looking for a crew. Have any men here worked on ships?"

"I have."

So, Jon had been right. "Would you be interested in working on a ship again?"

"A ship? What ship?"

"I need men who know how to sail," Jon said. "Fifteen good men who you trust. Can you get them?"

Ayuba studied Jon's face. Then he glanced at Nanny Quassy.

She said, "He's a good boy. He's a friend."

Ayuba said, "We will meet you in the hurricane shelter in ten minutes." Then he walked away.

What if he raised the alarm? He'd been told to lock Jon up. Was he trustworthy? He glanced at Nanny Quassy. But her eyes were on the road, and she gulped, visibly.

"Oh merciful God, here comes trouble," she said.

A familiar figure on horseback galloped headlong up the hill. He looked bigger than ever as he scanned the crowd of running slaves. Jon's heart plummeted.

Blackheart Bill!

"Quick, inside!" Jon pulled her into the hut and locked the door.

Nanny Quassy grabbed Jon's arm. "Who's on that horse?"

"Blackheart Bill. The pirate that's chasing Florabelle and me."

"Out the back window with you," she said. "He hasn't seen you yet. Run. I'll tell him you were never here. Get to the shelter."

"But Florabelle, I have to warn her!"

"You leave that to me."

"But—"

"No buts. You'll never find her on time. I'll warn her. Now go!"

"Thank you, Nanny Quassy. I don't know how to ever repay you."

A horse whinnied. A loud pounding sounded at the door.

Blackheart Bill's raspy voice rang out. "Open up, or I'll break the door down. I know you're here, Jon, and you're a dead man."

Jon's heart almost leaped out of his chest.

"Go!" Nanny Quassy pushed him to the hut's back

window. "Quick, my friend. Run straight ahead, don't stop."

Jon wiggled through the back window and charged through the fields of sugarcane, hoping he was headed toward the hurricane shelter.

Sure enough, he burst from the fields and saw the shelter door. But when he opened it, he could only gape in shock.

Instead of fifteen would-be sailors, Ayuba had brought what looked like over a hundred slaves and convict laborers.

Ayuba seemed apologetic. "They all want to escape. Can they come?"

The workers stood silent, their eyes on Jon. It was almost as if no one was breathing.

Head spinning, Jon looked at the desperate men. How on earth could he escape with so many?

Then he remembered the horror of being Blackheart Bill's slave.

"Yes. Yes, of course." He went to the iron grate and lifted it. "This escape tunnel leads about five miles to the coast. There's a cave at the end. You're in charge, Ayuba. Wait there, stay quiet."

Ayuba ushered the crowd toward the tunnel. Faces tense, the workers climbed into it, one after the other.

Jon opened the hurricane shelter door a crack. Where was Fortune? He couldn't leave without her.

Hurry. Please, hurry up!

There came the sound of running feet. What if it wasn't Fortune? What if Blackheart Bill had tracked him?

A small figure dressed in breeches and an oversized

canvas jacket stumbled toward the shelter. It was Fortune followed by Nanny Quassy.

"Hurry up!" Fortune gasped. "What are you waiting for?"

"You," Jon said.

"Get inside, Florabelle." Nanny Quassy's dark eyes were glazed with fear. "Hurry."

"Come with us, Nanny," Fortune begged.

Nanny Quassy hugged her hard. "I'm too old, my child. Visit me again when it's safe. Now go! Run!"

20

C rammed into four borrowed longboats, Jon, Fortune, and the crowd of slaves pushed silently away from the pier.

They'd made it this far. Soon, they'd be home free.

"Wait! Stop!" A dark silhouette ran down the jetty.

Jon dug in his oars, desperate to escape.

"It's me, Cook," the figure shouted. "Blackheart Bill is after me. He knows I saw him kill a mate and bury the treasure."

Jon's heart flipped. "Hurry! Swim out!"

"I can't!" Cook wailed. "I'm too fat."

"You can. Swim. Quick!" Jon cried.

From out of an alleyway charged a huge, muscled pirate on horseback. Blackheart Bill! Jon stiffened in horror as the towering villain thundered along the jetty, cutlass in hand.

Fortune shouted. "He'll kill us! Row, Jon. Row!"

Cook leaped off the jetty and into the ocean. Splashing and gulping down water, he screamed. "I didn't see you bury the treasure, Blackheart Bill. I didn't see you kill no one. Jon didn't neither. I never meant to tell the Captain."

Jon groaned.

With a roar of rage, Blackheart Bill dismounted and leaped off the jetty into the sea. Waving his cutlass, he sloshed through the knee-high waves. "Ye has been blabbing yer big toothless mouth off, Cook. Ye lying sea weasel."

Blackheart Bill reached Cook and shoved his head underwater, yelling. "Ye dirty liar!"

Jon had to get to his friend, or he'd perish!

Cook struggled, while Blackheart Bill wore a terrible shark smile.

"Hey, Cookie, the mermaids are awaiting," Blackheart Bill crowed. Heart thundering, Jon raised his oar. He stretched out and brought it down hard. The oar just skimmed Blackheart Bill's shoulder.

The pirate whirled around and let out a triumphant roar. "The devil's brought you back to me. You're a dead man!"

Maniacal eyes gleaming, the giant pirate clamped a hand on Jon's boat. He raised his gleaming cutlass and brought it whizzing down. He was about to split Jon in half.

For a moment, Jon went blank with fear. Then, his survival instincts kicked in. He blocked with the oar. The cutlass thunked into the wood and stuck there while the oar slammed into the pirate's ear. The whack made Blackheart Bill's eyes roll back in his head.

He groaned and went under.

"Cook," Jon cried, fearing Blackheart Bill wouldn't stay down for long. "Grab my oar, hurry!"

Cook just floated there, eyes staring up out of the sea.

Jon leaped into the water, grabbed Cook by the shirt,

and hauled him to the longboat. Two slaves reached over and pulled Cook up over the side.

Before Jon could join him, an awful splash made his heart clench. Like a sea monster, Blackheart Bill rose up out of the ocean.

"You're dead, ye nasty little bilge rat!" the pirate screamed.

The ragged crew of slaves started splashing their oars, blinding Blackheart Bill with seawater.

Arms hauled Jon aboard.

Fortune shouted, "Row!"

With oars churning through the waves, they headed into the bay.

Cook puffed like a whale. "The rum made me do it, Jon. That devil's brew loosened me tongue. I told Captain Morgan about the buried treasure. I told him Blackheart Bill killed our mate. We saw it all with our own eyes, I told him. You, me, and Fortune." He groaned. "Row, my boy, that's a good lad. He'll kill us."

Jon and Fortune shared a look. Then they shook their heads. Cook wasn't the brightest star in the sky, but he was an experienced sailor, and that was what they needed.

Cook squinted at the crowd as if seeing them for the first time. "What's the game, m' lad? Where are we going with this ragtag bunch, if you don't mind me sayin'?"

Jon gave a laugh. "This here's our army."

At this, the crew cheered.

"We're all getting away," Jon said. "I'm planning on borrowing a fair sailing ship."

"A fair sailing ship, hey?" Cook said.

Jon pointed to the red-gilded merchant ship. "That one."

"We're borrowing a ship?" Fortune said. "That's your plan? Holy cow! And she's flying a red Spanish pirate flag!"

"She's not really Spanish. She's an English merchant trader—stolen just like our merchant ship was stolen. When she sailed in, she was flying the Union Jack."

"Oh dearie me." Cook wrapped his arms around his chest. "Blessed Saint Nicholas, protector of the desperate, save us. Spanish pirates?"

As they drew near, the small fleet fell silent. Creaking at anchor, the tall ship sent shadows across the longboats. They bumped up against its hull, the water glowing orange in the early light.

Who knew how many pirates had been left to stand guard?

Jon led the way up the rope ladder, followed by Cook.

A sole guard lay snoring on deck with an empty bottle of rum clutched in one fist.

Clearly, they weren't expecting an attack from the sea. Everyone was fighting at the fort.

Jon and Fortune tiptoed up to him. Jon clamped a hand over the pirate's mouth as he snorted awake, and Fortune tied his wrists and ankles. Cook gagged the man with his headscarf.

"That'll keep 'im quiet, hey?" Cook whispered.

"Good work," Jon said. "Come on, let's see who else is on board." Heart jabbering, his ankle still sore, he limped toward the main cabin.

From inside, a drunken voice suddenly sang out, and another laughed.

Jon paused. He motioned over the side to Ayuba.

Silent as shadows, Ayuba and their raggedy crew

swarmed up the rope ladder. Faces tense, some carried oars while others grabbed the pikes propped against the mainmast.

Jon pointed to the cabin, where the drunken sailor had begun singing a Spanish song.

Horribly aware that he and the others had no muskets, he threw open the cabin door.

Inside, seven Spanish pirates were busily downing rum and delicious-smelling food. They gaped at the crowd of wild, half-naked men.

Eyes bulging, a Spanish pirate lunged for a nearby pistol.

Jon dove, too. He got it first and aimed. "You'll save yourselves a lot of pain if you leave the ship," he said. "Longboats are waiting for you down below."

"English swine," the Spaniard roared. "I spit on you."

"Spanish scum!" Cook yelled. "Scabby cockroaches!"

The rest of Jon's crew tried to cram themselves into the cabin.

A yellow-haired convict worker grabbed a pistol and shouted, "String the Spanish rats from the yardarm," wildly firing into the ceiling.

For a terrible moment, Jon pictured dozens of men fighting to their deaths.

Fortunately, the Spanish pirates realized they were outnumbered. Cursing, they fled the ship.

Jon, Fortune, Cook, Ayuba, and their crew cheered.

"We're free!" the men shouted.

"We're free!" Jon and Fortune shouted.

Like famished wolves, they descended on the food, devouring the chorizo sausage, fried squid, crispy pork rinds, and fried potatoes. More food was brought up from the hold. Cook, smiling widely, handed out jars of rum all around.

"Ooh, delicious!" Fortune crammed figs and sugar pastries into her mouth.

Jon banged a pike on the table. It was time to go—before Blackheart Bill mustered a boat or the Spanish pirates returned.

All ears turned to listen.

"Welcome, gentlemen," he said. "I am Jon Fincham, the guardian of this fair ship for the next four weeks. Cook, over here, is your captain."

"Captain," Cook said, bowing and blushing. "Listen to that, me, a captain!"

"And Ayuba is the quartermaster," Jon said.

Ayuba nodded, also clearly pleased with his role.

"We sail for Charles Town in the Carolinas," Jon said. "Those who wish to journey all the way may do so. Those who wish to stay in the Caribbean, we'll drop at Hispaniola, where you can hunt wild boar, forage for fruit, and live as free men."

The crew cheered. Perhaps they didn't care where they were going, as long as they were free.

Jon's ankle began to ache, but he couldn't relax just yet. His gaze flicked toward Port Royal. The Spanish they'd sent ashore would be raising the alarm. Time was ticking away.

"Does anyone know how to navigate?" he asked.

A gray-bearded man held up his hand. "Long ago, I worked as a navigator, sir."

Jon sighed in relief. "Excellent."

Cook shouted, "All right, me hearties, if ye knows how to set sail, raise your hand."

Dozens of work-worn hands went up.

"Yer all with me. Let's get this beauty moving."

Fortune said, "Just so you know, I'm not going to be the barrelman."

"Of course not. You're co-boss of the vessel," Jon said. "With your own cabin."

Fortune grinned. "Yes! My own cabin! Now you're talking."

Jon grinned. "Hoist the sails and raise the Union Jack. Let's get out of here."

The red-gilded ship, flying England's Union Jack, sailed swiftly out of the harbor.

One week later
The Atlantic Ocean

Hands firm on the helm's wheel, Jon gave a contented sigh—ocean life was sweet. The red-gilded ship, her full sails billowing, cut through the spray-swept sea.

"Can you believe it?" he said to Fortune. "Not one stormy day. Just blue skies and swift winds."

"It seems the saying is all wrong."

"What saying?" Jon asked.

"All that malarkey about girls and ships," she said.

Jon laughed. "You're right."

They glanced around at the happy crew. Cook had been teaching them pirate songs. They sang as they caulked, cleaned, spliced, and polished.

> For his work he's never loth
> And a-pleasuring he'll go
> Though certain sure to be
>   popped off
> Yo, ho with the rum below!

Jon felt glad, but he couldn't help thinking of their treasure, which they'd lost in their mad escape. Fortune had given the few coins she'd saved to her nanny so that Nanny Quassy could buy her freedom. They'd managed to find a bit of silver aboard, and they'd divide it amongst everyone when they reached Charles Town.

Cook approached. "You've a fine ship here, m' lad. The life of a privateer is a good one."

"Nah," Jon shook his head. "We both know it's not my ship. I'm returning her to the harbormaster in Charles Town. He'll get her to the merchant trading company who owns her."

Cook looked mournful. "I hope they reward us well, m' lad. We saved her from Spanish pirates, we did."

"I hope so," Jon said.

"What'll you do after you hand her over?" Cook said.

"I'll go home. I can't wait to see my parents. I'm sure my pa will take me whaling this year. I bet you can come with me."

Cook's eyes lit up. "Whales, you say? Do you think so? Fortune, will you come along, then?"

"Whales?" Fortune turned slightly green, the way she used to when they'd first met.

Jon suspected he knew the answer.

But Cook rubbed his hands together. "Sounds like high adventure."

"I think I'm going to hang up my sea-legs," she said. "Maybe I'll set up a sailing supply shop."

"A shop?" Jon said. "You can't afford that!"

"Oh, yes, I can." She drew a leather pouch from around her neck, opened the top, and poured out three giant gems into her palm.

"You saved some of the treasure!" Jon cried.

"One stone for each of us," she said. "Big enough to make our dreams come true."

"I'll open me own restaurant tavern," Cook said, hugging his gem to his chest.

Jon's eyes shone as she handed him a glittering, fat stone. "I'll learn more about navigating. I'll buy a fishing sloop. I'll call her the *Fortune.*"

Fortune grinned. "That works for me."

The three hugged one another.

Jon said. "I can't wait to tell Ma and Pa about all this. Being captured? Fighting in battles? Digging up treasure? I can still hardly believe it myself. But we did it all. And by our amazing skill and cunning, we escaped pirates in the Caribbean!"

10 Fun Facts About Pirates

1. Some say pirates wore eye patches to keep one eye adjusted for seeing in the dark below deck.
2. Although most pirates thought women were bad luck, some women were fierce pirates and captained their own ships.
3. Captain Kidd is one of the only pirates known to have buried his treasure
4. Every pirate ship had its own rules or *Pirate Code.*
5. One of the most common rules was *no fighting aboard!*
6. The word *pirate* comes from *pirata*, which means sailor or sea robber in Latin.
7. Pirate treasure wasn't always gold and jewels. Often it was cloth, food, leather, lumber, and supplies
8. A Jolly Roger is the skull-and-crossbones flag, but not every pirate ship used this emblem.
9. Pirates were punished by hanging in public to warn others from following in their footsteps!
10. While pirates and parrots are often shown together, no pirate is known to have kept a parrot aboard ship.

Download this book's study guide at:
scottpetersbooks.com/worksheets

- Ahoy, Matey – Hello, friend
- Avast, me hearties! – Stop, my friends!
- Shiver me timbers – Yikes or Whoa
- Thar she blows – A whale sighting
- Scurvy Dog – A pirate insult
- Blimey – Yikes or Whoa
- Scallywag – Rascal or Rookie
- Booty - Treasure
- Maroon – Leave someone stranded
- Walk The Plank – To be forced to walk off a ship's plank and jump into the 'drink' or ocean

Parts of the Ship

- Bow – Front of the ship
- Stern - Back of the ship
- Port - Left side of the ship
- Starboard - Right side of the ship
- Bulwark – Railing around the outside edge
- Deck – Floor
- Poop Deck – The raised deck at the back, where the steering wheel is located
- Bilge - Bottom 'pit' of the ship
- Hull – Bottom and sides enclosure of the ship
- Mast – A vertical pole used to hang the sail
- Crow's Nest – A lookout platform on the mast

BOYS CAPTURED BY PIRATES

In the Golden Age of Piracy, boys on pirate ships ranged in age from 9 to 19. Some were captured and forced to become pirates or pirate slaves, while others chose to join the pirates. Some escaped and some didn't.

Here are three:

In 1814, fourteen-year-old **Charles Tilton** was an apprentice on a whaling vessel when pirates raided the ship. Captured, he worked on French pirate Captain Jean Latiffe's ship for six years and they became good friends. When he was twenty, Charles sailed his own schooner up the Texas Trinity River and returned home.

Sixteen-year-old **John Julian**, was a Central American boy captured by pirates in 1717. John became a skillful ship's pilot and guided the pirate ship, the *Whydah*. During a terrible storm, the *Whydah* sank. Only John and the ship's carpenter survived. Tragically, John Julian was captured and sold as a slave. He made numerous attempts to escape. During one escape, he killed the bounty hunter pursuing him and he was executed.

In 1716, nine-year-old **John King** and his parents were passengers on a merchant ship sailing the Caribbean. When pirates raided the ship, John suddenly decided to join the pirates. He told Captain Black Sam that—unless they let him join their crew—John would kill his own mother. John won the battle of wills and went off with the pirates. A few months later, he drowned in a shipwreck. In 2006, archeologists exploring the 18th century shipwreck discovered John King's leg bone, silk stocking, and boot.

CAPTAIN HENRY MORGAN

Captain Henry Morgan, who lived from 1635–1688, was one of the most successful pirates and privateers of all time.

From his base in Port Royal, Jamaica, Captain Morgan raided settlements and shipping on the Spanish Main and became extremely wealthy.

In 1671, he plundered Panama, the richest city in the western hemisphere, and returned in triumph to Port Royal. He believed he was acting with the approval of the British Crown. However, while he was off looting, Spain and England signed a peace treaty.

The Spanish were angry because they felt the treaty had been broken. To appease them, England's Governor Modyford arrested Captain Morgan. The pirate was summoned to trial in London.

In a surprising turn of events, when he reached London, he was treated as a hero. The English people loved him. He was praised by the government, knighted by King Charles II, and made a baronet. He ended up serving as acting governor of Jamaica from 1680 to 1682.

In 2011, archaeologists from Texas State University diving near the Lajas Reef, Panama, discovered a large section of hull believed to be part of Henry Morgan's sunken flagship, the *Satisfaction*. A treasure trove of artifacts included cannons, swords, barrels, and chests.

THE I ESCAPED SERIES

I Escaped North Korea!

I Escaped The California Camp Fire

I Escaped The World's Deadliest Shark Attack

I Escaped Amazon River Pirates

I Escaped The Donner Party

I Escaped The Salem Witch Trials

I Escaped Pirates in the Caribbean

MORE BOOKS BY ELLIE CROWE

Surfer of the Century, The Life of Duke Kahanamoku

Nelson Mandela, The Boy Called Troublemaker

The Story of Olympic Swimmer Duke Kahanamoku

SCOTT PETERS

Mystery of the Egyptian Scroll

Mystery of the Egyptian Mummy

Meet America's Presidents! 2-Minute Visits

JOIN THE I ESCAPED CLUB

Get a free pack of mazes and word finds to print and play!

https://www.subscribepage.com/escapedclub

BIBLIOGRAPHY

Cruickshank, Brig-General Ernest Alexander, *The Life of Sir Henry Morgan,* The McMillan Company, Canada.1935

Earle, Peter, *The Sack of Panama*, Viking Press,1972

Esquemeling, Alexander, *The Buccaneers of America*, 1684, Scribner, 1898

Hilton, Evelyn Gill, *Kidnapped by Pirates*, Trafford Publishing 2010.

Paine, Ralph, *Blackbeard: Buccaneer*, Penn Publishing Company, 1922

Pope, Dudley, *Harry Morgan's Way*, Alison Press 1977

Pyle, Howard, *The Book of Pirates*, Dover Publications

Stevenson, Robert L., *Treasure Island*, 1883

Tey, J., *The Privateer*, The Macmillan Company.1952.

CPSIA information can be obtained
at www.ICGtesting.com
Printed in the USA
BVHW070600190421
605286BV00001B/35

9 781951 019198